To DANA,
GOD Bl...
Marty Wilson

To Dana " My Bis Cousin"
I hope you enjoy the
book — Love You —
Jerry

THE GODMOTHERS

A NOVEL BY

Stacey Eleuterius Barber

Crooked Letter
PUBLISHING
D'Iberville, MS

ISBN: 978-1-7320653-0-7 (Hardcover)
ISBN: 978-1-7320653-1-4 (Paperback)

Library of Congress Control Number: 2018932542

Any references to historical events, real people, or real places are used fictitiously. Names, characters, and places are products of the author's imagination.

Front cover image by Marty Wilson and Mippi the Dork.
Book design and edit by Darnell Fayard Sheffield

Printed by Bookmasters, Inc. in the United States of America.

First printing edition 2018.

Crooked Letter Publishing, LLC
3179 Mallett Road
D'Iberville, MS 39540

www.crookedletterpublishing.com
www.thegodmothers.biz

~For my Mom and Dad~
who have always told me I could do anything
I put my mind to... even writing a book.

~Acknowledgments~

I am very fortunate and honored to have
the same group of friends since grade school.
We spend as much time together as possible.
Even though some of us live in different states,
they are my support system and my cheerleaders.
There is a little of each one of us in
Gina, Carlita, Francesca, Antonella and Adrianna,
a.k.a. *The Godmothers*.
I love my girls!

Thank you to the best editor in the world,
Darnell Fayard Sheffield,
my fellow D'Iberville gal,
and to my cousin,
Tammy Murray Chapman,
who dropped everything and took over
to help get this book published.

~CONTENTS~

1. LIPSTICK LOUIE   3

2. BOUDREAUX'S NEW SHOES   7

3. TIME FOR THE BIG EASY   16

4. LET'S GO   25

5. BOOM   56

6. GINA GETS A PLAN   63

7. SURPRISE   75

8. PHASE ONE COMPLETE   81

9. BILOXI BOUND   86

10. MAKE ME OVER   96

11. BEAU CHIC APPAREL   100

12. SUPERMODELS   104

13. FOOLED BY THE POOL   111

14. HIT REWIND   120

15. SHE'S THE MAN   127

16. EVER HEAR OF A BRAZILIAN?   135

17. PRETTY WOMAN   151

18. HE'S NO RICHARD GERE   159

19. TRAINED CIRCUS MONKEYS   170

20. BODIES, BAYS, AND BAYOUS   178

21. IF LOOKS COULD KILL   182

~PREFACE~

They say, this is a man's world, but I proved them wrong. I surprised everyone, even myself.

You see, as mafia wives, our job was to raise kids if we had them, keep the house running smoothly, always stand by our husbands, and never ask questions. It's a *what we don't know won't hurt us* kind of thing. I was never very good at the do not ask questions part. I paid attention and when the time came, it paid off. Now, I am running the show. I will tell you my story. However, if you breathe a word to anyone, I will send my girls to keep you quiet, if you know what I mean. My name is Gina. They call me GiGi. I am the new "Boss," and this is my story.

1. LIPSTICK LOUIE

You could hear all of the noises of the city. It was a cool, dark typical New York spring night. Horns were blowing, sirens blazing, and alarms sounding off. These were faint sounds in the background. The alley was dark, lit by a dim streetlight flickering. A buzzing sound could be heard, just like in old movies.

Sally, Nico, Drago, and Marco were in the alley. They were roughing up another character who thought he was smarter than they were. Every week, some young punk thought he could take over the business. Sally had very little patience for anyone who tried to disrupt business, or take what did not belong to them. They were attempting to convince this man to tell them what they wanted to know and warned him what would happen if he did not. Luigi was normally the one who handled the rough stuff, but he was nowhere in sight.

The man was begging and pleading for them to stop, but they were dragging it out longer than usual, hoping Luigi would show up. Once he realized they were not going to stop no matter what he told them, he knew he was not going to make it out of the situation. He tried to go out with all the sarcasm and cockiness he could muster.

Sally had finally lost interest in anything else the man had to say.

"Get rid of him," he told Marco.

Marco did not like the sound of that. He was walking over to him when he could hear Luigi running up and apologizing for being late to the party. He was slicking back his hair and tucking in his shirt, the men all noticed.

Luigi immediately got into the tough guy routine and walked over to the man. He nudged him with his polished, winged tipped shoe. He was tough and strong. His forearms were large and thick like Popeye. He grabbed him with one hand, lifting his body up off the ground by his collar. His legs lay limp on the ground. He knew exactly what to do.

Marco was still fussing at Luigi. Although he was handling what he needed, Marco wanted to know where in hell he had been. Marco was not afraid to get his hands dirty but always preferred that Luigi handle this type of thing, unless there was no other choice. The man on the ground noticed Luigi had red lipstick all over his lips and neck. He referred to him as 'tough guy' and asked if he was wearing lipstick.

Luigi simply responded, "Maybe it is, but it's the last lipstick you'll ever see."

He then leaned down and gave the man a big kiss on the forehead with a puckering sound, transferring some of the red lipstick from his lips to the man's forehead.

Luigi was still apologizing to Sally for being late as he was dragging the man down the alley to finish him. "Sorry Boss."

A couple minutes later, there was a single shot. Luigi walked toward the guys and out of the shadows.

Luigi got into his car where Sally was waiting for him. Marco, Drago, and Nico got in the other car and took off.

"Well Lipstick Louie, you almost missed all of the fun. Where were you, and where did you get the lipstick?" Sally asked, teasing him about the lipstick but wanting to know where he had been.

Luigi looked in the rearview mirror. His face immediately turned red, almost as red as the lipstick on his neck and smeared on his lips. He knew it was there after they called it to his attention, but he did not realize how bad it was. He immediately pulled the pressed, monogramed handkerchief from his pocket and started wiping it with vengeance. He almost took off the top layer of skin.

"Boss, I've got to give up these crazy young women. I'm ready to find a normal woman. Tonight, this one took the cake. She was riding on the crazy train. Hell, she was the conductor of the crazy train. Man." Sally shook his head and cranked the car.

Sally was giving him a hard time, but he wondered how bad she could have been. He had more lipstick on his face than a hooker on Saturday night in the red-light district. His interest peaked. He had to know why she was so crazy.

Luigi always dated young, immature, starry-eyed girls, who liked the excitement of his lifestyle and even some crazy ones. He did like the finer things in life. For this to be the one to make him give them all up, Sally had to hear this story. Luigi agreed to tell him, but he made Sally promise to forget the conversation ever happened.

As the car pulled away, Luigi began to tell about his spiritual experience. All that could be seen were taillights. All that could be heard was the sound of Sally laughing hysterically as they disappeared into the night.

2. BOUDREAUX'S NEW SHOES

June 16th started like any other day. All of us girls were meeting for lunch. Carlita, Francesca, Antonella, and I were planning to go shopping and have a little fun together. We did this regularly.

It was 10:00 a.m., and Francesca used her cellphone for a four-way call. They always wanted to talk on the morning of our day together to make plans, select a lunch location, and talk about what they were going to wear to build excitement. Everyone was getting dressed in their spring clothes, no coats, and smiles on their faces, knowing we were headed out for our girl's day.

Each of us have very different personalities, but we have been together for so many years that we are like sisters. We get along well, with the exception of the occasional rift, but they are always short lived.

Let me tell you a little bit about my girls.

I have always been the serious one of the bunch. My personality has always been a little bossy, as a big sister would be. I was usually the instigator for whatever we did, good or bad. Somehow, I was always able to talk them into following along with me.

Carlita was very reserved and smart. She was the organizer. She was more like the middle child, except there are four of us. If we had a charity event or one of the kids had something, she would handle the financial part of the project. Whatever I could dream up, she made it happen. She had a good sense of humor but did not have an outgoing personality. She liked to stay under the radar but always got things done.

Francesca was very sweet and very boisterous. She was always energetic and rowdy at times. She was willing to do whatever anyone needed of her. She could be tough when needed.

Antonella was a character. She was rarely serious and always entertaining. Antonella and I are first cousins and close in age. She keeps us together and in harmony. She is a peacemaker.

Antonella and Francesca are usually the life of the party. They keep us from getting to serious. Antonella and Francesca fight for the baby sister role.

Walking down the New York City streets was always fun for us on a beautiful day. We felt like an older version of the girls from *Sex and the City*. Of course, I was Carrie Bradshaw, in my mind anyways. We were heading to one of our favorite restaurants. It had a great private, glassed in patio off to the side of the main dining room. We could spend as much time as we wanted.

"Table for four please, in our favorite spot," I said to the host.

The host smiled and grabbed menus. He led us to the back, set the menus down, and smiled.

"This is perfect. We can make all the noise we want. It's a girl's lunch. We plan on having many martinis and enjoying this beautiful spring day.   We might even break out in song at some point," Antonella told him.

"Ladies lunch and lots of liquor. Sounds like trouble to me! I guess we're going to have to keep all eyes on you ladies today," he said as the waiter approached. "Looks like you've got the perfect waiter. I think he can handle you all," he said

"You don't know the half of it." I agreed and winked at both of them.

The waiter was a young handsome man. He had blonde wavy hair, big brown eyes to die for, and rosy, plump lips and dimples you could dive into. He was handsome, but also had just enough swag and sarcasm to make his personality perfect for this kind of day.

"How about I get some martinis over here to get this party started," he said.

The drinks started coming and so did the laughs. I knew we were getting louder with each sip, but it was one of those days. We wanted to have fun.

Antonella was famous for telling her *Boudreaux and Thibodeaux* jokes. She could voice the accent perfectly. She did not spend much time in the south or Louisiana, but she had it down perfect.

Antonella channeled her inner Cajun, "Let me tell you about Boudreaux's new shoes." Everyone leaned in.

"Boudreaux bought a brand new pair of black, patent leather shoes and he was so proud of them. He took them straight home and spit shined them up so good he could see his reflection in them.

He picked up the phone and called Marguerite. 'Mais Cher, Marguerite, I done got me some new shoes, yeh. Let's go to the dance tonight.'

Marguerite said, 'Okay Boudreaux. That sounds good. I'll see you tonight.'

They got to the dance. They were dancing. Boudreaux stuck his foot up under her dress and said, 'Marguerite, dat sure a pretty pair of pink drawers you wearing.'

'Boudreaux!' she exclaimed. 'Now how do you know what color my panties are? '

He said, 'don't you worry about dat.'

The next night they went back to the dance, 'Mais char Marguerite, dat sure a pretty par of blue drawers you wearing tonight.'

'Boudreaux, I swear, I don't know how you know dat,' she said shaking her head.

The next night, he slid his shoe under her dress, just right and all of a sudden, he grabbed his chest and fell to the floor.

Marguerite knelt down beside him and said, 'Uh huh, I done fooled you Cher. Tonight I didn't wear no drawers.'

He said, 'oh thank God, I thought I had a crack in my new patent leather shoes."

Everyone was telling stories and jokes, one after the other. We laughed hysterically. Even the waiters would come over just to listen to Antonella tell her jokes.

I certainly was not as funny as Antonella or any of the other girls for that matter. I am a bit more serious. However, I had a story to tell. One Sally had told me about Luigi.

I was not supposed to tell, but it was the funniest thing I had ever heard, except maybe for Antonella's jokes.

I began to tell them about the night Luigi got his nickname, Lipstick Louie. It was a typical Luigi Saturday

∞11∞

night. He was out with the latest string of twentyish year old girls. He wowed her with the limo, fancy restaurant, and bubbly champagne. Usually by the end of the night, they went home with him. This night had a little bit of a twist.

Everyone was drawn in, listening and waiting for the rest of the story or the punch line. They were not sure at that point. They knew it had to be good for me to be telling a secret.

"Things were heating up. The lights were dim, the champagne bottle was upside down in the bucket on side of the bed, and half-full glasses were on the nightstand. Clothes were all over the room, and music was playing in the background, Deano I am sure. Sally said the girl was a freak. Luigi told him she was going crazy all over him. Then, all of a sudden, she jumped off him, grabbed a pillow from under his head, threw it on the floor, kneeled on it, cupped her hands, and started praying. Buck-naked! She was praying out loud for forgiveness for what she was doing!" I exclaimed.

All of the girls died laughing loudly, so loud you could hear us all over the restaurant. I was usually a bit more reserved than the rest of the girls, but I could turn it up when needed. I also had a flare for the dramatics. I could exaggerate a good story.

"She said out loud, 'Dear God, please forgive me for what I've been doing and for what I'm about to do. Amen!'

And she was looking up at Luigi while still on her knees. He was in shock and just staring at her.

There was an awkward moment of silence. She kept looking at him as if she were waiting for something. Then she raised her eyebrows at him and repeated to herself, 'Amen.' She tilted her head as if to ask... well? Not knowing what else to do, he finally said 'A...Amen'. She immediately tried to jump back on, but she hit the bed and missed him all together. He jumped up like a jackrabbit and said, 'OH HELL NO! NOT AFTER THAT! NO WAY!' He grabbed his Saint Christopher medal that was around his neck, kissed it, and made the sign of the cross. All of this, while backing away and just about running from her as he picked up his clothes one piece at a time, covering himself," I paused.

Everyone could hear our hysterical laughter throughout the restaurant. Even the waiter came over this time to see what was so funny.

"He told Sally, that's it, no more. He was quittin' crazy. He said he was waiting for her to throw holy water on him, or something. He kept looking for lightening to strike him down all night. He was so serious."

Every time we mentioned Luigi's name, we started to giggle about the story I told.

"Sally said he looked like he meant it. Luigi said he has had a serious girlfriend for a while. He did not want to tell anyone until he knew for sure that she was the one. Her name is Adrianna Romero. Last night Sally asked that we start including her in on our girl's outings.   He said she's different from his typical young, dumb, and perky twenty year olds."

Adrianna was younger than the rest of us, but still in her forties, very well built, and always looking like a million bucks. She was smart and sassy, which was exactly what he needed. He would have been bored with anything less. Sally said that Luigi even called her "the one." That was a big statement coming from Luigi, since he had never settled down with anyone. He always had many women, and they did not stay around long.

"Romero doesn't ring a bell. Is she even Italian? Do we know the family?" Carlita asked.

"I don't think so. I think it's French," I said.

I told them everything I knew about her, but it was not much. I knew if it got serious, Sally and Drago would have her checked out. They would not spend any time on her until they knew for sure. If they checked out all of Luigi's girls, it would be a full time job. They would do what was necessary when the time came.

We thought if we accepted her into our group, he would feel more comfortable and would finally settle down. We were sure we would like Adrianna and were happy for Luigi, but it was always difficult for us to let someone in from the outside. We are a family, maybe not by blood, but by choice. You know the old saying, you can pick your friends and your nose, but you can't pick your family? Well we did.

When you are accepted in, there is only one way out, if you know what I mean.

There had been four of us girls for such a long time. It was going to be strange having someone new in the mix. When all of us would go out to dinner we would take turns having two dates, our respective husbands and Luigi. Rarely ever, did he bring the twenty something tarts to dinner with the family.

Before we knew it, we had spent all afternoon in the restaurant and had too much to drink. We skipped the shopping all together. Truth be told, we did not like to go shopping anyways. We just used that as an excuse to get together. We rarely ever made it to any stores. This day was no exception.

We finally decided to call it an afternoon and head home to cook dinner for our husbands. I decided since I had so much fun at lunch that I would keep the merriment going. I had music playing, a fresh bottle of wine opened, and I was dancing around the kitchen like Ginger Rogers.

Sally walked in and dropped his brief case. He grabbed my hand and twirled me around the kitchen without missing a beat.

"Must have been a good afternoon?" he asked as he kissed me on the nose while he had me in a dip.

I smiled at him with a mischievous grin. We sat down at the table and I told him about the stories we told. Well, most of them.

3.   TIME FOR THE BIG EASY

As usual, it was Monday morning, and the guys were sitting around a dark room, talking business, checking in on all of the locations, playing cards, and doing who knows what else.

All of the power was around the table. The table was round, and the light in the room was dim. The room looked the same for as long as I could remember. If tables could talk, oh the stories it could tell. There have been many decisions made around it.

The power around the table changed through the generations, but the table and the room stayed the same. As girls, we were never allowed in. It was a boys club. I can only go from memory on how bad the room really looked, but it was bad the time I went in. I remember Sally brought me with him one night after hours to pick up something he needed. He was breaking the rules by letting me even walk through the door. He was still young and powerless. He was missing a few links in the chain of command. He was too young and naive to care.

Dishes were cleared so they could conduct business. The lingering aroma of Italian food and of Uncle Hugo's famous pizzas bubbling in the brick oven permeated throughout the restaurant. Uncle Hugo let the guys use the back room of his restaurant to work. Even before Sally's Dad, Giancarlo Madrina, a.k.a. Carlos, and his brother, Uncle Tony, were in charge, the Capone family were using the back room as their office. They eventually bought Uncle Hugo's restaurant and paid him to run it so they could use the back room.

The Madrina family needed legitimate businesses to show income. All of the guys put money in a fund called "family money." They bought other businesses as well. We had all types, from restaurants, to dry cleaners, and even an art gallery.

There was a big speakerphone in the center of the table. Even when technology changed, the speakerphone stayed the same. It even had a cord. The size of it took up the entire center of the table. If it wasn't broken, it didn't get fixed.

Fridays were always the same. They would have a call to get reports and updates on business in other cities. Sitting at the big table every week is my husband, Salvatore "Slick Sally" Madrina, also known as "The Boss." I call him Sally.

Sally had been in charge for almost twenty years. He had done a good job, but he still did things the same way they did decades ago. He was old school, and he did not like change or technology.

I told him all the time, "Sally, you need to make some changes to work smarter, not harder."

His response was always the same, "Baby, you just have fun and let me handle the business." It always drove me crazy.

Next to Sally at the table was Drago Madrina. He was Sally's right hand man. We called him "The Dragon," because of his piercing eyes. They were always red from staring at numbers all day, and he never slept. The legend was he once scared someone to death by his stare. I am not sure how true that is, but it was their story, and they were sticking to it. He was a serious man, like most bean counters. He was not going to win any personality contests, but he was smart, did not say much, and loyal to the family.

Drago's dad sent him to college to keep him away from the family business. His dad and Sally's dad were cousins and worked side by side for years. He did not want his son to follow his footsteps. He thought college would keep him away from Sally and New York.

Drago met Carlita in college. They both had accounting degrees, but Carlita never worked. After college, they married and moved back to New York. It did not take long for him to become Sally's right hand man. Carlita and Drago were very much alike, very smart, analytical, and conservative. Carlita is not outgoing, but she has a good sense of humor.

Nico "The Nose" Zunino got his nickname because he could smell trouble a mile away and could always tell when someone was up to no good. He was intense. His role was the in-house detective and bloodhound. He could always uncover a problem or find out any information needed. He was the man who made things go away or cleaned up someone else's mess before it became an issue. He was a problem solver and had no problem getting his hands dirty. His methods could sometimes be questionable, but he always got the job done. He was Luigi's backup on the rough stuff.

Francesca is Nico's wife. She knew what Nico did and turned the other cheek. She understood what needed to be done. She is sweet, but could also be tough in her own right.

Luigi Caruso was next. He was quite the ladies' man and went through young women like fresh underwear. They loved him. He was charismatic and handsome. His looks could be deceiving. He could turn on the charm then turn it off in an instant when he needed to get serious. He handled the rough stuff and was as tough as wet leather. He was a lover and a fighter.

Then, there was Marco Bellini, "The Preacher." He was easy going, but when he got on a roll, he could talk for hours and sounded like he was preaching. He was fun loving, and boy, did he like to eat. He was serious when he needed. He kept things running smooth. He was a big man and a little overweight. Most people liked to deal with Marco. He could talk people into doing what he wanted without having any trouble. The running joke was that people did what he wanted them to do, so he would stop talking.

Antonella is my cousin and we were close growing up. Sally and I introduced her to Marco. It was love at first sight. They married within six months of their first date. They both loved to eat, sing, and have fun.

Nico reached over to the center of the table and turned off the mute button.

He greeted everyone on the call and asked, "How we doin' in Vegas?"

He then proceeded to each of the representatives for each city. Vito responded, Neely responded, and so on.

Everything seemed good. All money was on its way. Every location was paying and cooperating, every place but New Orleans.

Lil' Rocco was in charge of operations in New Orleans. He was Sally's nephew. A typical family member who got a job he did not deserve. He only did the minimum requirements. He thought he was entitled like a democrat on the first of the month. The guys worked with him to try to make it better, but something was never right. It was always excuses, one after the other.

"So, are you sure everything's good in New Orleans?" Sally asked again. Five minutes of endless excuses followed.

Sally's eyes looked around the room as he shook his head. He knew the response he was going to get before Lil' Rocco even answered. He looked at Nico, because Nico always knew. He winked back at Sally and shook his head.

"Sure Uncle Sal. I've got it all covered. I know I did not send in as much as usual, but I am working on some things. You know the economy down here ain't so good."

Sally's response was always the same, "Okay kid." However, this time he knew that he had to do something to check it out further.

Sally had a round face and big round eyes. He was very animated, like his personality. His controlled expressions gave away his thoughts when he wanted them known. He also had a great poker face and smiled, even when he was mad. This made most people nervous.

"Okay boys, everything sounds good. Rocco, call when you have your update. Same time, next week." Sally said. He dismissed everyone on the call.

Drago reached over and hung up the call. He asked what everyone around the table was thinking. None of the guys were buying Rocco's story. They knew he was up to something. Everything else seemed to be in order, with the exception of Rocco. They were not sure what he was up to, but something did not feel right. It was more than his typical laziness.

"Boys, it's time to head down to the Big Easy to see what our boy is up to. Let's tell him we are bringing the girls for a little vacation, so he doesn't suspect we are on to him. A little trip down south will be great for everyone. It will make him nervous, I'm sure. He's already a nervous kid. He's been that way since birth," Sally said.

They immediately started making plans for the following week. They did not to waste time.

When Lil' Rocco found out that the guys were coming to his city, he became very nervous. He was afraid they were on to him. He did not want them to know he was suspicious of their trip, so he tried his best to play it cool.

That night, Sally came home and told me he was taking me on a vacation. I was at the sink in the kitchen cooking dinner. He came up behind me and kissed me on the neck.

"GiGi, baby, I have a surprise for you. We are going down to New Orleans. I asked everyone to join us for a little fun. It will be a great trip and we deserve it," he said as he was leaning around me to see my expression from behind.

I looked at him in disbelief and a half smile. All I had to do was look at Sally, give him a look, and raise one eyebrow. He was well aware I knew there was more to the story. There was always more to the story with Sally.

"Okay, so you called me GiGi and baby in the same sentence? Now I know you are full of it. No work at all?" I asked with a smirk on my face.

He smiled back with a guilty grin. "Well, mostly play. I'll have to go check on what Lil' Rocco is up to. Ya know something's just off with that kid right now. My nephew is giving me heartburn."

I agreed, but tried to get him to commit to some play. I even made him shake on it. We shook hands. Then he grabbed me and gave me a big kiss to seal the deal.

Sally asked me not to tell the girls about Rocco. He needed everyone to think the trip was just for fun. He did not want Rocco to get suspicious.

Sally's phone rang.

He apologized for the disruption of our kiss, but saw it was Luigi calling.

"Hello, hello. His phone is in his pocket again, no one is there. Hello. Hello," Sal said louder.

"Damn Luigi," growled Sally. "One of these days that damn phone is going to get him in trouble."

It happened so often that neither of us paid it much attention.

I was suspicious of the reason for the trip but excited. I put it out of my mind and wanted to give Sally the benefit of the doubt. Maybe they could take a vacation, but I knew better.

"Don't worry about that," I said, referring to the butt dial from Luigi as I grabbed his phone and set it on the table.

"When do we leave for our trip?" I asked.

"Next Friday," he said with a smile and still looking over at his phone.

"Sounds great, can't wait."

4. LET'S GO

"Wake up Sally. It's time to get up. We're going to New Orleans today," I said excitedly.

He had not moved a muscle yet. I reached over and grabbed the blankets and pulled them off him.

"Get up. Time to get rolling," I said in my deepest Sally voice. It always made him laugh when I spoke to him in his own voice.

Usually, Sally was up and gone before my feet ever hit the floor, but I was ready for the trip.

"Okay babe, I'm awake." Sally slowly rolled over and rubbed his eyes, as he tried to wake up. He smelled the coffee I had set on his nightstand.

"Come on. Coffee in bed. What more could you ask for? I have got your clothes all laid out, and your bag is all packed. Let's get rolling! You're taking me on a trip," I said and laughed as I pulled the covers off him the rest of the way.

"And I set your briefcase by your luggage so you don't have to sneak it," I said jokingly.

He smiled with his eyes still closed. "Baby you're the greatest, and you're always a step ahead of me." He was acknowledging I had him all figured out.

"Two," I said as I was walking out of the room.

"Maybe three." I laughed as I walked down the hall.

We met at the private airport and began boarding the plane. There were ten of us.

Luigi introduced Adrianna to everyone. He looked very happy and proud to have her with him. We had heard all about her, but this was the first time we had actually met her. It must have been intimidating, but she handled herself well under the circumstances. It was impressive.

Carlita came over to me at the steps of the plane and leaned in as everyone was boarding.

"What's going on? What are they up to with this trip? Are we supposed to believe this is just play and not for business?" she asked.

I grinned back at her. She and I were usually on the same page. She had them figured out about as well as I did.

"I haven't figured it out yet, but I'm sure you're right," I responded.

"I'm sure, but what's the harm in us letting them think that they are smarter than us," she joked.

We laughed, climbed the steps of the plane, and sat in our seats.

The plane was beautifully decorated. You could smell the new leather on the cream-colored plush seats. It had inset lighting and the burl wood trim around the arms of the chairs and on the sidewalls of the fuselage was gorgeous. There was a full bar area, a large bathroom, and two seating areas separating the guys from the girls on trips.

Luigi boarded to find a wrapped package in one of the seats with his name on it. He picked it up and sat down. He looked puzzled and looked back at Adrianna, as if to ask if it was from her. She shook her head, shrugged her shoulders, and looked as puzzled as he did.

Everyone else filed in and took their seats.

A soft voice came over the intercom. "Good morning everyone. We will have some hot coffee ready after takeoff. Buckle up and enjoy your flight."

Luigi unwrapped his gift, laughed, put his hand over his face, and lowered his head down. His face was as red as a beet. It was a book of prayers and a bottle of holy water. He held it up for everyone to see. Everyone laughed, except

Adrianna. Of course, she had not heard the story of the crazy girl who proceeded her. No one confessed to giving the gift.

Looking over at Sally, Luigi said, "You can't be trusted." He smiled and pointed his finger at Sally as if he were in trouble.

Sally turned to me smiling and shaking his head because I was not supposed to tell anyone the story and neither was he.

As usual, almost as if we had assigned seating like in grade school, the guys sat at the front of the plane, and the girls sat in the back.

I sat down first, and everyone else sat around me.

"First things first," Antonella said to Adrianna, "tell us how you met our Luigi."

So not to miss a single detail of the story, everyone leaned in.

Adrianna began to tell us about a date she was on one Saturday night. They had dated a few times, but it was nothing serious. She had already grown bored of the man but had not figured out how to blow him off yet. They were having dinner in a crowded hot new restaurant in the city.

The place was loud and the acoustics were terrible. Everything was hard and white. There was nothing to absorb the chatter in the room.

They were seated at a two-top table in the middle of the room. All of the two-tops were close together. By the time her food arrived, she had totally tuned out her date and was more interested in listening to the conversation at the table next to her. Of course, you might have guessed, Luigi was at the next table with whatever twentyish year old he was dating that week.

She began to listen to him turn on the charm but sadly most of his conversation and jokes went straight over his date's head. He was talking, and she was tweeting.

"At one point, I died laughing at one of his jokes. He looked over at me, then at his date, then back at me and rolled his eyes. I was embarrassed, but maintained eye contact. The conversation shifted to him. I was doing all of the talking. My date sat there like a bump on a log and his could not put her cellphone down between selfies. She spent so much time tweeting about how much fun she was having that she forgot to actually have some.

The waitress came over and placed a check on Luigi's table and then on ours. While my date was paying our check, I excused myself to go to the restroom. I motioned for Luigi to do the same. I waited outside the restroom to see if he would follow. He did.

I handed him a piece of paper with my phone number on it and told him to call me after he dropped his daughter off at home," Adrianna joked.

Everyone laughed as she continued her story. She said he closed his eyes and shook his head, but he was intrigued by her confidence and sarcasm. He knew she was making fun of him dating this young girl.

She said he called that same night, and they talked until daylight.

"And the rest is history. We have been together every day since," she said as she sat back in her seat.

All of us looked at her with admiration as she had finally done something no one else had ever been able to do. She made Luigi a one-woman man.

After her story, the conversation shifted to the trip and making plans. We began making lists of all of the fun places we wanted to go.

Antonella started by suggesting Café Du Monde.

Francesca chimed in, "Antoine's and Commander's Palace for the famous Jazz Brunch. Oh, of course, shopping on Magazine Street and in the French Quarter."

Adrianna was smiling as they spouted off their lists.

"Sounds like a lot of calories," she said looking frightened at the thought.

We looked at her as if she had just said a terrible thing.

Antonella said jokingly, "Damn, you figured out our evil plan. We are going to force you to gain a few pounds this week. Skinny people make me nervous!"

We all laughed.

Antonella continued, "I especially love walking around the French Quarter and listening to all of the great musicians. Some of the best musicians in the world play on the streets of New Orleans."

"Sally's grandmother lived next door to Doopsie, which was a famous New Orleans musician. His son is Rockin' Doopsie. He and Sally are great friends. I'm sure he has called him, and we will get to see him play while we're here," I told the girls.

Carlita tried to bring Adrianna back into the conversation. "Adrianna, Luigi told us that you like to shop. So we know you want to go shopping."

Carlita leaned into the isle to see him. "Luigi, I hope you brought your wallet?"

We all laughed. Luigi winked, nodded, and tapped his wallet in his pants pocket, as if to say, *I got it.*

"Adrianna, tell us what else you like to do. Oh, do not forget the Riverwalk and Bourbon Street. They are must do's," Carlita said before Adrianna had a chance to answer.

"What about Pat O'Brien's with the dueling piano bar? I love that place. We have to do that," Francesca interrupted.

"See Adrianna, we're going to do a few things other than eat while we're here," Carlita said.

"Would you guys slow down and give her a chance to answer?" I had to interject.

Adrianna finally spoke, "How about the casino? Don't they have casinos in New Orleans?"

"I think if we are going to a casino, we need to drive to Biloxi and spend a few days there as well. The casinos are great on the Coast and they have quite a few of them to choose from," I explained.

Everyone thought that going to Biloxi was a great idea.

"After we go to all of these great restaurants, maybe we should walk to Biloxi," Adrianna said jokingly.

Everyone laughed as the excitement was building. It was nice to see that she had a sense of humor.

Antonella was always the funny one of our group. "Nah, let's not get carried away."

The guys heard the laughter and wanted to know what was going on. They were all talking quietly in the front. The louder we got, the more distracted they seemed to be.

"What's all the laughter and plotting going on back there?" Luigi could not stand it.

He had a big smile on his face, as though he wanted to be a part of whatever we were doing, instead of the serious conversations going on in the front of the plane.

"We were thinking that we should go to the Biloxi casinos, while we're this close. What does everyone think?" The guys turned to me. I had their full attention.

Nico answered quickly, "Sure. Great idea. Whatever you girls want to do. This is your trip."

He leaned back in to the guys. He told them they could check out the Biloxi operation.

Sally leaned over and winked at me. He suspected I suggested Biloxi to help him. I knew he would want to go check it out as well, since we were close. I smiled back at him, winked, and immediately brought my attention back to the girls.

I know how things work, probably more than any of the other wives, because I see what Sally has to do to keep everything running. It is how he stays on top. I payed attention and studied what he was doing and why. I always made mental notes in my head of how I would have handled a situation and if it differed from what Sally had done. It was for my own entertainment.

I was watching Adrianna and was surprised how well she handled the pressure of meeting all of us for the first time. She carried herself well and had a confidence about her. I could see what drew Luigi to her.

"Coffee, juice?" The flight attendant came around taking orders.

The flight went by quickly with all of the planning and talking we were doing. Before we knew it, the intercom clicks on with the voice of the pilot. He instructed us to fasten our seatbelts for landing.

"Welcome to New Orleans," he announced.

The limo was waiting for us on the tarmac next to the plane. Everyone jumped in. It was a bit crowded, but we just scooted in close together.

The driver had a thick Cajun accent. "Welcome to New Orleans. I hope ya'll had a good flight. Ladies, I have not had the pleasure of meeting any of you, but I have driven your husbands for years. I have heard a lot about all of you. My name is Alphe' Arceneaux."

Sally was glad to see him. He added, "That's right. Alphe' has always taken good care of us. That is why we are going to have him take you girls around. We will take one of his other cars. Alphe', I want our girls to be taken care of while we are here. Sing a little for them too. Girls, wait until you hear him sing. He should've been a singer instead of a limo driver."

"Good thing I'm not, you might be driving me around instead of the other way around," he joked at Sally. "I will take great care of your girls. And Sal, my little brother Alcide will be your driver."

"That sounds good. He will take us wherever we want to go, unlike you," Sally responded jokingly and continued. "You've been with us far too long. You do not listen anymore. That's the problem with our relationship."

Everyone laughed.

"Hey, I just try to keep you out of trouble while you're in town. Not that you look for trouble," he said quickly when all of us girls turned to look at him, then to our husbands.

"Trouble just seems to find you sometimes." The more he said, the more eyes turned to him. "Im gonna stop talking now." He said with a smiled.

"Well, we sure have heard a lot about you too," I said trying to give him a little relief.

"Everything, except how handsome you are. They left that part out," Francesca told him. "We can't wait to get you alone so you can tell us what our husbands have really been up to when they were all alone in New Orleans over the years."

"It will be my pleasure ladies. To drive you," he quickly inserted into the conversation.

All of the guys turned to Alphe'.

"What?" they all asked in unison.

"No, Nooooo. I meant to drive you, not tell secrets," Alphe' said loudly.

All eyes were on him.

"Not that there are any secrets," he added.

Alphe' turned red in the face. Everyone laughed at his embarrassment. He put his face in his hands.

"Boy, this is going to be interesting. Let's change the subject. Please. Ya'll are killing me. The weather should be nice while ya'll are here. Our first stop is the famous Café Du Monde for some fresh beignets and café au lait. Then to the Roosevelt Hotel in the Quarter to check in," Alphe' said

It was a short drive from the airport, especially with all of the excitement and conversation.

"Here we are," Alphe' declared as we pulled up.

You could smell the chicory from the brewing coffee as soon as the limo door opened. The smile on Sally's face said it all. Café Du Monde and New Orleans hold such fond memories for him.

"The green and white awnings make me smile every time I come here," Sally said as he was stepping out of the limo.

Marco was already rubbing his belly and licking his lips when he smelled his first whiff of the aromas.

"The beignets make me smile," he responded to Sally as he made a mad dash for the counter while leaving the rest of us at the limo, as if we were in slow motion.

The restaurant was packed. Everyone was enjoying beignets. The kids all around had white powdered sugar all over their faces. We ordered and sat at a large, black, wrought iron table and took in the atmosphere.

There was jazz music playing in the background and big ceiling fans whirling overhead. Chattering and laughter added to the atmosphere.

Everyone started licking their lips as the waiter came to the table with trays of beignets. Marco's face lit up like a kid on Christmas morning. He looked like one of the surrounding kids eating his beignets. He had as much powdered sugar on his shirt as he had on his beignet. Some of the kids had white and green paper Café' Du Monde hats on. We had to get one for Marco as we left.

Alphe' had already pulled the car around and was standing with the door open to greet us.

"So, did everyone enjoy that? Marco, it certainly looks like you did. They even gave you a hat. Did you have some café au lait? It's my favorite." He continued as we climbed in the limo, "The secret is the chicory and the hot milk. My Maw-Maw would sneak a lil' to us kids when we stayed with her. We called it coffee milk. I think of her and smile every time I have a cup. Back then, kids could not go down the block for a Starbucks coffee. Our parents did not allow us to have coffee. They told us it would stunt our growth, but Maw-Maw was cool. She let us get away with anything and everything. We thought we were grown when she let us have a sip. Well, here we are, the Roosevelt."

The doors opened and there were bellmen at every door. One of the door attendants greeted us at the limo. He used words like ma'am, sir, and thank you. He told us how happy he was to have us visiting New Orleans and The Roosevelt. It was always easy to tell when you were in the south. He actually meant every word he was saying.

"There's nothing like southern hospitality," Sally said as he exited the limo. He continued, "You won't find any friendlier, sincere, more considerate, or down to earth people anywhere. I love it down here. It takes my blood pressure down a few notches the minute I arrive."

Sally started the tour as soon as we walked in the door of the hotel. He told us about a great bar called

Sazerac, which was located in the lobby. The Sazerac Bar is famous. There have been many famous people stroll in for a Ramos Gin Fizz. It is famous and infamous.

We decided to check in and relax a while. Then, we would meet at the Sazerac at five for cocktails and head out for an early dinner at Antoine's. Everyone arrived at the bar all rested and dressed for dinner.

Sally said, "Come take a walk with me girls. These walls are lined with great photos of people enjoying themselves in the Sazerac. Take a look. This is Louis Armstrong, and here is President Reagan. Here's Al Pacino. There are politicians as well. This is a great, long, running Senator from Louisiana named Bill Cleveland having drinks with his wife and some friends. Even present day celebrities visit this bar when they come to New Orleans."

"Hey, what do we have to do to get our photo on the wall?" Antonella asked.

"Well, I don't know. As many times as we've been here, we haven't made the wall yet, thank goodness," Sally laughed and winked.

The cheers started with Sally. "Here's to a great trip. Cheers."

I said, "Here's to New Orleans."

"Here's to the Sazerac," said Luigi.

The night continued. We had one of the best meals at Antoine's. I know Sally says that every time we eat there, Commander's Palace, Mr. B's, and even when we get a

Lucky Dog on the street. You really cannot miss. The food is just incredible.

Marco was chuckling. "Now that's my kind of dinner. I love New Orleans. After this meal, we'll need to sleep it off to be ready for brunch at Commander's Palace in the morning."

We were having none of it. No sleep for us yet. We rarely got the guys away from work. We were taking full advantage.

"Sleep? No way! We are heading to The Dueling Piano Bar at Pat O'Brien's," Francesca ordered.

The guys had their bellies full and were ready to call it a night, but they gave in agreed to take us out.

"Okay Alphe'. We lost a bet and the girls won," Sally joked.

"Take us to Pat O's. That's where the girls want to go," Sally said as they drove away and headed to Pat O'Brien's.

"Here we are. This is as close as I can get you tonight. The streets are blocked off," Alphe' informed us.

Walking was fine. After all, we were New Yorkers. We walked. After the dinner we had, we needed it.

The city was alive. Lights and music were everywhere. Contrary to what you hear, it is not really Mardi Gras every day.

There were bars, restaurants, galleries, and souvenir shops. We decided to dash into a souvenir shop as we passed it. We tried on hats, boas, and beads. We danced to the music, and everyone walked out wearing something fun. We looked like we fit right in on Bourbon Street, except we were sober, and of course fully dressed.

We fooled around the Quarter and had loads of fun. We finally made it to Pat O'Brien's and The Dueling Piano Bar for music and dancing.

"Here we are. I love this place!" Antonella yelled above all of the noise.

We walked in. The music was crazy good. Everyone in the bar was singing along and having the time of their life. They formed a line and danced around the place. They grabbed us one at a time to join the line. Before we realized, it was already almost midnight. Time passed so quickly.

"Come on. Let's get out of here. I have a surprise for ya'll," Sally said with excitement.

"Ya'll," everyone laughed.

"You're already getting an accent after one day," I said jokingly.

"Yep, it comes pretty easy for me," Sally said as he smiled.

"Here we are," Alphe' said as he pulled up to Storyville. "After I park, I'm coming in. I don't want to miss this!"

Sally had called his old friend Doopsie to see where he was playing, so we could meet up with him and listen to his band, Rockin' Doopsie and the Zydeco Twisters. Zydeco music filled the room with energy. Sally and Doopsie had known each other since they were kids. He had a reserved table in front for us.

Doopsie finished a song and stopped the music.

"Wait, wait, wait. Hold up everybody. I just saw some old buddies walk in," he nodded to Sally.

He continued, "Now let me tell ya'll a story. When I was about eight years old, we had a next-door neighbor that had grandkids. They came to visit every summer. She had a boy and a girl. We played together just about every day. We even did chores together.

One day the little boy Sally," he pointed to Sally in the crowd and all eyes turned to us, "had a great idea. See Sally had a little sister named Dena. She followed us everywhere. Where we went, she wanted to go, no matter what. She would knock on my door and ask *can wittle Doopsie tum out to pway?* She was so cute.

Well, this day we were playing in the yard. Sally got an idea. He said *I'll be right back.* A couple of minutes later, he came running out with a big umbrella and Dena.

You see, the day before this happened; we had been raking up leaves from all of the big oak trees in the yard. There were piles everywhere. My Dad was having some work done on a room. There were ladders, tools, and all kinds of things laying around that kids could get into. Before I knew it, he had all three of us on the roof. He wrapped Dena's hands around the umbrella and threw her off the roof into one of the big piles of leaves. He said he wanted to see if she could fly like that Mary lady on his little sister's movie. I still remember my Mama and his Maw-Maw running to try and catch her.

We didn't sit down much that day," he said rubbing his backside.

He continued, "There's a lot more stories where that one came from. I'm gonna sing a brand new song for my old friend Sally. It's called *I'm a Music Man*. I hope ya'll like it."

We stayed and enjoyed the music. Doopsie and Sally told more stories about their summers in New Orleans together into the wee hours of the morning after the bar closed and the lights came on. We finally headed back to the hotel for a much-needed good night's sleep.

"Maybe tomorrow after our brunch, you girls should go have some time at the spa or an afternoon of shopping. We will go golfing, get a shave, and do some guy stuff," Drago suggested.

I know guy stuff was code words for work and checking on Lil' Rocco to see what he has been up to, but I did not comment. The girls seemed to be having too much fun to question anything.

The next morning, everyone met in the lobby and immediately jumped in the limo. We were ready to enjoy the famous jazz brunch at Commander's Palace. We were not used to those late nights of partying, so we were dragging a bit.

"We need a little hair of the dog to get us going," Marco said.

"Hair of the what?" Adrianna asked. "I don't know what that means."

"You'll see, soon enough," Marco playfully said.

We were seated in the main dining room where all of the action was. There was a jazz quartet walking around singing. Spicy Bloody Marys and Mimosas passed around the table. The smells of the atmosphere were heavenly.

Everyone looked at Marco as he read the menu and licked his lips. You would have thought he had not eaten in days.

"My Maw-Maw had a black lab named Gumbo when I was a boy. When she got ready to feed him, his mouth would start pouring water and his tail would wag so fast, I thought it was going to fall off. That's what Marco looks like right now. I can't see his tail, but I bet it's wagging," Sally joked.

The waiter came over with the trays of Mimosas and Bloody Marys.

Marco held up his Bloody Mary and looked over at Adrianna, "Hair of the Dog."

I still do not think she understood what he was suggesting. He had too much wine the night before and the old saying is 'only more alcohol will cure the headache.' Luigi was leaning in to explain.

Everyone ordered and enjoyed each other. The quartet started singing. Marco sang along. When they heard him, they came closer and nudged him to stand up. All of the patrons in the restaurant went crazy and started clapping. Marco jumped up, stood in the chair, and started singing louder. His cheeks were rosy from the Bloody Marys and a little embarrassment. Eventually, Antonella stood up and finished the song with Marco. She did not mind the attention. She was always the class clown. They both love to sing and have fun.

A restaurant photographer came around to the tables taking photos. He took one of Marco standing in his chair with his arms stretched out wide.

"That photo will make the wall of fame in the front entrance," the photographer said as he continued to snap photos.

He smiled as he took another of Antonella standing next to Marco. Everyone in the restaurant looked at them enjoying every note.

"Ya'll look like ya'll are having too much fun. I think ya'll need another pic to remember this day," the photographer said.

Of course, they sold these photos, so he was certainly going to keep clicking.

"Okay, say cheese," he yelled over the restaurant music and noise.

Everyone retorted, "Cheese!"

"We'll take five of those, one for each couple!" Marco yelled back.

Adrianna was quick to correct him. "Make that six. I would like one as well."

The others were married couples; of course, one would do for them. That was not the case for her and Luigi.

Luigi corrected her as he motioned to the photographer to come back to the table.

"Five is enough," he said as he stood up looking at Adrianna.

Luigi moved his chair back and pulled a small box out of his pocket. He turned to her and got down on one knee. She immediately covered her face with her hands in shock.

"Baby, I never thought I would say these words, but I've never been happier in my life and I have to ask you, will you marry me?" he asked.

"Yes, yes, yes!" She kneeled down on the floor, faced him, and kissed him.

She leaned back away from him.

"Now give me that ring," she said jokingly as he slipped it on her finger.

Everyone in the restaurant clapped again. The photographer was snapping shots of our table the entire time.

"Champagne over here!" Sally yelled to the waiter. "And go buy every photograph and put them on our bill!"

We sang and danced all the way out of the restaurant and back to the cars. We were stuffed again.

"Well, I'm full again. I have never had this much good food in my life. It is a good thing I do not live here. I would be in trouble," Adrianna said.

There were two limos waiting outside the restaurant. Alphe' was in front of one and his brother, Alcide, was in front of the other.

The guys kissed us goodbye. Sally was still dancing and holding my hand. He twirled me over to Alphe' and blew me a kiss goodbye. Alphe' opened the door for me. I looked back and blew him a kiss back. He disappeared into the limo.

Luigi was the last to get into their car.

He stepped back out and yelled, "As they would say in New Orleans, ya'll pass a good time today. Yeah?"

We laughed and waved. Our limo pulled away in one direction and they went in the other.

Alphe' had a bottle of champagne chilling in the limo for us to keep the merriment going.

"I understand congratulations are in order." He was looking at Adrianna in the rear view mirror.

"Yes," she said with excitement while admiring her beautiful ring and showing it off.

The toasts started all over again.

I said, "To Luigi and Adrianna!"

They held up their glasses and took a sip.

"And to us!" Francesca lamented.

Everyone drank again.

"To my fiancé'!" Adrianna threw in.

"And to our husbands!" raised Antonella.

Another sip.

"To our diets we will have to start on Monday." Adrianna always had to joke about diets.

We were tipsy and giddy. We toasted to anything and everything.

"To the best driver ever!" Carlita yelled raising her glass to Alphe'.

Everyone raised their glasses again. Alphe' smiled and lifted his coffee cup back to us.

The other limo had a different vibe. I am sure Sally was all business as soon as they pulled away.

"Okay, now we can do some business. Did you call Lil' Rocco yesterday to get the meeting set up?" Sally asked Marco.

"Yes. It is all set up. We are meeting at a restaurant on the outskirts of town called Grosso's. It is only open for dinner, so we will not be disturbed. Lil' Rocco set everything up for us already," answered Marco.

They arrived and Lil' Rocco was waiting outside to greet them as they were getting out of the limo.

"Hey Uncle Sally, Marco, Luigi, Nico, Drago. How was brunch? Sorry I could not make it. I had some last minute things to take care of for our meeting," he said nervously.

"No problem kid. It was great. I'm as full as a tick," Luigi said as he rubbed his belly.

They were keeping everything social and slowly gearing up for the meeting. They had fully decompressed after leaving New York and had some fun for a couple of days.

Lil' Rocco lead them through the empty restaurant and to the large room he had reserved in the back.

He seemed a little nervous and the guys noticed. They started the meeting off light, as if their visit was completely spontaneous and nothing was wrong.

"So Lil Roc, did Luigi tell you he popped the question at lunch?" Drago asked, trying to make some small talk.

"Congratulations," he said half- heartedly, as he shook his hand to congratulate him.

They had a little more light conversation and then got down to business. As they dug deeper into Lil' Rocco's books, he obviously grew more nervous.

"Where's all the money Roc? I have looked at your books and have been watching you. There's a lot missing," Nico said firmly.

It was always one excuse after the other with Lil' Rocco. He thought because his Dad was Sally's brother, he was entitled to more than anyone else was.

"Nico, I think you're missing some things. It is all there. Maybe I did not send you everything. I will check after our meeting and get back with you. It has been crazy here lately. I'm sure it's just an error," he stuttered while trying to explain.

He knew there was no buy in around the table by the expressions on their faces, or lack thereof. Voices got louder and tension grew around the table. The conversation heated up. The more questions Drago asked, the fewer answers he had. Lil' Rocco was talking in circles. He felt the pressure from Drago. Drago looked over at Luigi. With one slight head nod in Lil' Rocco's direction, Luigi got up, slid his phone in his back pocket, and began walking around the room. He paces when he gets mad or anxious. He leaned over Lil' Rocco with an arm on each side of him and his hands on the table to apply a little intimidation.

"Why don't you check now," he ordered him as he leaned against him with his chest against Rocco's back, pushing him a little forward.

"Okay Luigi. I have some files and my laptop in the car. Let me make a call. I will go out to the car and get everything. Everyone relax and I will have some drinks brought in. Be right back."

At that, Lil' Rocco got up and excused himself for a few minutes. When he left the room, Luigi sat back down and shook his head.

Luigi said, "These kids think they can pull one over on us. They think with their fancy new iPhones and computers that we won't understand. They just don't get it. We've already forgotten more than they will ever know," he laughed as he said it.

Meanwhile, the girls and I were still out enjoying the day. We decided to get out and walk. We meandered in and out of shops and galleries. Adrianna's phone rang as we were getting back to the limo. It was Luigi. She had his photo on her iPhone screen when he called.

She stopped to answer it and put it on speakerphone.

"Miss me already?" she asked with a smile as she answered.

The rest of us were leaning in to listen in on the call.

"Hello?" She could hear voices, but he was not on the line.

She started to hang up, but she heard a female voice.

The server had walked in to bring the drinks. "Rocco said to come in and get your drink orders. Can I get anything for anyone?"

We were all listening and watching her face when we heard the female voice.

Adriana was young and knew of Luigi's reputation.

"Sounds like they have women with them. I'll kill him!" Adrianna said with anger.

Sally spoke up, and they could tell he was speaking to the server. "Thanks doll. That will be all for a while. Why don't you go have a break and keep everyone outta here for a bit, so we can talk business."

As he dismissed her, they continued talking. She nodded as she left, closing the door behind her.

I had to step in. "Wait, it was the waitress. Calm down." I reassured her.

I realized at that moment Adrianna had a lot to learn. It was never good to be emotional and reactive. The control was something that came with age and self-confidence, which we were ahead of her on both accounts.

I tried to hang up the call, but the girls realized the guys were talking business. There was no golf in their immediate future.

"Let's go get them. They promised they would not work," Adrianna said strongly.

Carlita who understood as well as I did of what had to be done to keep everything running chimed in, "Let's go get them and drag them out of wherever they are. They said they were going to play golf! Nico left his book in the safe so I wouldn't get suspicious."

"Sally left without his briefcase too. Maybe they stopped by to see Lil' Rocco on the way to the course," I said.

I knew better, but never wanted to let the girls know Sally confided in me at all or that I knew what was happening and they did not.

I had to act as surprised as the rest of them, but if they had paid more attention, they would have noticed the three-hundred dollar dress shoes the guys were wearing. There were no golf shoes or clubs in sight.

Antonella leaned in to Alphe', "How can we find them?"

All eyes turn to Alphe'. He could feel the stares and looked at us in his rearview mirror, but did not respond.

I did not know where they were going. I never asked. I could not do or say anything to appease the girls. They were determined to find them and drag them out of whatever kind of meeting. I knew they would not be happy with us. The only thing I could do was try to warn Sally.

"You ladies know I can't tell you where they are. Ya'll are gonna get me into big trouble," Alphe' told them while trying hard to stick to his orders of keeping the girls busy all day.

"You're gonna be in even bigger trouble if you don't tell us," Francesca told him.

Adrianna thought for a moment and then interrupted. "Luigi and I have the 'find your iPhone' app on our phones. I can find them. Give me a minute".

"Find a what?" Francesca asked.

Adrianna said, "We can find them ourselves. Let me show you. That will show them to tell us a fib! With a man like Luigi, I figured the only way I could keep tabs is to put a tracking device on him. I took him to the vet to get one of those bar codes implanted I had for my puppy, but they would not do it. I figured this was as close as I could get."

Everyone laughed, but paid close attention to what she was doing.

She looked up from her phone. "Stick with me ladies. I'll teach you some new tricks."

Maybe she could teach us old dogs some things. I paid close attention, as I did with most things. I figured this could definitely come in handy. She was younger than the rest of us and more familiar with technology. She began working on their location.

"Ah ha! Found them. They are at 274 Grosso Road. Alphe', sounds like it's time for a detour," Adrianna exclaimed.

"Are you sure you want to do this? They are going to be awfully mad at us if they are there in a meeting." I had to ask one last time to make sure they thought it through.

"Okay, Okay, Okay. I know where they are. I'll take ya'll," he said as he reached for his phone to try to warn them.

Alphe' was relieved it was Adrianna who gave up the location, and he did not have to.

"We're going to drag our husbands away from work and make them relax. They need it, and we deserve it for putting up with this kind of thing," Carlita said in her matter of fact tone.

Grosso's was about twenty minutes away from where we were. Alphe' started to drive.

"Boy are they in trouble," he laughed, "And me too, for bringing you to catch them in the act." He shook his head.

They turned off the highway. You could hear the gravel road beneath the tires. The last five minutes of the drive were on this road with not too much in sight. It was off the beaten path, for sure. There was no danger of us running into them by accident. I'm sure that is why they chose it.

Alphe' was trying to send a text to the guys to warn them, but we were outside the city. The area did not have a good signal. He crossed his fingers and hoped the text went through before we got there.

His text read:

Warning, Incoming!! The girls found ya'll, better run while you can! We're on our way, lol.

He hit send. *Not Delivered* showed on the screen. He hit send again and hoped for the best. He certainly was not going to win any races as slow as he was driving. He was trying to give them plenty of time to get away before we arrived.

Alphe' nervously spoke, "Well, here we are. It does not look like much, but it is a great restaurant. It is called Grosso's, named after the Boss of all Bosses from Louisiana. It is a great place for people like your husbands to do business and not have to worry about who is listening. They hold a lot of business meetings for special groups during the day when it's closed," Alphe' explained slowly.

"Ladies, I'll wait here for you. Lemme get your doors first." He got out of the car and opened our doors.

He felt like he had to ask one more time. "Okay, are ya'll sure ya'll wanna do this?"

The girls were determined to drag them out of there. They promised us a vacation, and we were all going to get it.

I knew Sally was going to be upset, but I felt it was more important to go along so they did not find out Sally confided in me.

"Alphe', you wait here. We'll say we held you at gunpoint and forced you to bring us here so you don't get into trouble," Francesca told him.

5. BOOM

I winked at Alphe' and stepped out of the limo as the others were getting out.

We looked up and saw Lil' Rocco running out of the building. He jumped into his car. He was obviously in a hurry. He backed his car out fast.

We stood there looking at each other puzzled. Why was he running, and why did he peeled out? Rocks flew as he sped away. He was in such a hurry that he did not notice us in the parking lot.

Antonella looked over at Alphe'. "Alllllphee', did you warn them?" she asked as she put one hand on her hip and pointed a finger at him with the other.

Antonella was assuming that was the reason Lil' Rocco was leaving so quickly. She thought that maybe the others would be running out behind him. I knew better. Our husbands would not want to be busted for telling us a fib, but they certainly were not afraid of us and would not spend the energy to run from us.

Shaking his head no and laughing, he said, "I tried, but I'm not sure if it went through."

If Alphe' was not able to warn them, why was Lil' Rocco running? Maybe he got in trouble. If that was the case, it probably was not the best idea for us to show up unannounced.

The girls started putting it together that this was not just a vacation. There were some issues, and the guys were here to check on things, or maybe on Lil' Rocco.

Carlita looked at me. She now had her answer to the question she asked me while boarding the plane. I raised my eyebrows to acknowledge her. Carlita and I were usually on the same page and sometimes did not have to speak to understand the other.

She stopped and said, "Girls, maybe we shouldn't go in. The guys will not like it. That looked pretty intense."

Adrianna was determined. She was too starry eyed and in love to think about anything else. She really thought it was just a vacation.

Still playful, Adrianna pointed and shook her finger at Alphe' for attempting to warn them. "Alphe', you wait here. We're going in to see what's going on," she said to him as she was getting out of the car.

The rest of us were leery to go in, but still walked towards the building.

"Wait, were not going in Adrianna. We're going back to the car," I said as I glanced back at Alphe'. I knew this was a decision I had to make.

Just as we turned to go back to the car, Adrianna stood there with her arms out. She did not want to get back in the car. She started was the only one questioning me.

"We can call them. Now come get back in the car," I said.

Just as she turned to look back at the restaurant, there was a huge explosion.

BOOM!

The blast stopped us in our tracks and jolted everyone backwards to the ground.

Alphe' jumped out of the car and ran over to make sure we were okay. I got up and stood there in shock, staring at the burning building.

Adrianna tried to run towards the building, but Alphe' stopped her. He kept pushing us back. He was standing in front of us with both arms stretched out to stop everyone at once. We were all frozen. It took a moment for it to register what happened in front of our eyes.

"Nico!" Francesca screamed and cried.

Adrianna was crying and yelling. "Maybe they left already before Lil' Rocco!" She had desperation in her voice. "Alphe' check your phone. Did they get your message? Maybe they got your message! Please!" She begged him, looking for some reassurance from him, or from anyone. "Tell me they got your message, and they left before Rocco. Tell me!"

"Get in the car," I said very calmly. They all stood there like statues. "Get in the car, now!" I yelled.

I repeated to them to get in the car as I was helping Alphe' push everyone back.

"No! What if they are in there hurt? We have to go in," Antonella cried out. She and Adrianna attempted to run towards the building.

Boom!

There was another big explosion.

It knocked both Adrianna and Antonella completely off their feet. Alphe' ran over to help them up. He picked up Adrianna, carried her to the car, and put her inside. He then went back to get Antonella. She had been sitting on the ground watching the flames get higher. The building was collapsing with each small explosion.

"Get us out of here, Alphe'. Hurry!" I yelled.

Alphe' peeled out of the gravel parking lot as quickly as Lil' Rocco did.

Quiet sobs were the only thing you could hear. Each of us reached for our phones. The girls frantically tried to call their husbands to see if this was a horrible mistake. They were hoping and praying the guys had left the building. There were no answers. Each phone went to voicemail. I did not dial Sally's number. I sat with my phone in my hand, but I could not bring myself to call. I knew he would not answer this time, or ever again.

Dialing on her phone, Francesca said, "I'm going to call Lil' Rocco to see what the hell happened."

"No!" I yelled so loud it startled everyone. "He has to be part of this. Why was he running out of the building? We cannot call him until we figure out what part he played, and what we are going to do. Let's just get out of here and go back to the hotel to get ourselves together. We need to figure this out."

Carlita was nodding in agreement and grabbed Francesca's phone from her hands.

"This can't be. They must have left before Lil' Rocco. I am sure they are going to call us any time now. This has to be a mistake. We are overreacting. It just can't be," she kept repeating.

I immediately started giving orders. I asked Alphe' to take us to the hotel. I told everyone that when we got there, to walk in and not speak to anyone. No crying. We cannot let anyone know what is going on yet.

The twenty-minute drive back to town seemed like an eternity. Traffic in the French Quarter was busy. It took longer to make our way back to the hotel. I gave them my key and told them to go straight to my suite. I needed to talk to Alphe'.

Alphe' locked me in the limo and walked the girls inside. When he returned, he sat in the front seat. I sat in silence in the back. I had so many thoughts and emotions running through my head. I just had to sit alone for a few minutes. I could see Alphe' watching me from the rearview mirror. Neither of us said a word for over fifteen minutes. He let me process what just happened. He slowly opened his door, moved to the back of the car, and sat next to me. I looked at him and fought back tears. I felt a large one slowly fall down my cheek. He reached out to pull me to him. Even though I did not want to, I leaned in to his chest and let out a big sob. I abruptly pulled away, straightened up, and wiped my cheek. I could not show weakness.

I said with as much firmness I could muster, "Alphe', you can't tell anyone about this. I need some time to figure out what to do. Please keep this to yourself. They are gone. You know as well as I do. They are gone. They didn't leave that building."

He replied, "Yes Ma'am. Let me get you to your room. Do not leave the hotel without calling me to come take you wherever you need to go. We don't know what happened or who is behind it. Ya'll will be safe here tonight. I will be back in the morning. Call me if you need anything tonight. I will let you know when I hear from him. You know, the limo was not in the parking lot. There is a slim possibility they had already left. I will call Alcide to see where he is."

I replied, "Thanks Alphe'."

"Come on Gina, I'll take you up," he said as he reached for my hand.

6. GINA GETS A PLAN

I was standing at the door to my suite with Alphe'. I paused and looked at him with the key card in my hand, frozen, unable to put the key in the slot. My mind was racing in a thousand directions, and I was feeling every emotion possible. Alphe' had to take the key from me and open the door.

I walked into the room in a haze. It was quiet, even though the rest of the girls were in the sitting area. Alphe' came in to make sure everyone was okay.

He said, "I'm going to put the 'Do Not Disturb' sign

on the door and let the front desk know not to disturb any of your rooms. Do not let anyone in, no housekeepers, no room service, no one. Do not leave this room without me. I will be back first thing in the morning to help you. I wrote my number down on the pad over on the desk. Call if you need anything."

They nodded and Alphe' started to leave. His phone rang. It was Alcide. He went to pick up the guys and saw the building.

"Man, do you have any idea what the hell happened? I left to grab lunch and came back to the building and it's gone, burnt to the ground. Do you have the guys?" Alcide asked Alphe' with a loud and shaky voice.

"No they aren't with us. We saw it. We were there when it happened. I am with the ladies now at their hotel. Just get out of there before anyone sees you. I'll call you in a few," Alphe' replied.

I knew when Alphe' looked at me, it confirmed our greatest fear. His posture changed, and he was obviously deflated from the call. They were still in the building when it exploded. We had a conversation with our eyes. The girls still had a glimmer of hope, and I was not ready to take that away from them. However, I knew. I wanted them to have a little time for this to sink in before they had to deal with reality.

Alphe' hung up the phone. "Good night ladies. Try to rest. I'll see you in the morning."

No one spoke for a while. There were the occasional soft sobs. After a few hours, I figured it was time to take charge of the situation. I stood up.

"We need to have a plan." Everyone looked up, but still did not speak. I continued, "No one can know."

"No one can know what?" Carlita asked.

"That, that they are... gone." I could hardly get the words out.

I continued, "Alcide said he left Grosso's to pick up his lunch. The guys were not with him. They are gone. No one can know. We cannot let anyone know."

I took a deep breath, almost stuttering. Everyone seemed confused by my statement and looked at each other, then back at me. Since they were all looking at me as if I was crazy, I had to explain my thought process.

"Think about it. How will we live? We will be cut out of everything. There will not be any more money. All of the other families will be fighting to take over. We have to make everyone think they are still here with us, until we figure out what to do. We will just make this vacation longer than planned. Carlita, get a pad and pen. Let's make a list," I ordered.

"You're crazy," she said, laughing and crying at the same time.

Carlita got up and walked over to the desk shaking her head. I was sure she would be on board for whatever I wanted to do, but I did not quite have her there yet. It was too difficult for them to imagine, even her.

Adrianna yelled as she charged toward me, "How can you think about that at a time like this? Are you kidding me? What kind of person are you, worrying about yourself at a time like this? They are not gone! They are going to show up any minute, you'll see!"

Antonella jumped up and grabbed her before she made a big mistake. "Calm down. Hear her out Adrianna."

At that moment, everyone knew she was wrong. They were gone. They were not going to show up. They were not ever going to show up again.

I continued telling myself that she was young and in love. I decided not to overreact or have an issue with her.

"I'm the person you will be grateful to have later," I said as I walked over to the bar and poured her a drink.

"Think about it. We know how just about everything works. We know their routine. We have some of their stuff, computers, etc. We can figure this out. You all know I am right. We have to live. We have to make sure we are okay before we tell the world. As soon as we tell everyone, there will be a line to get us out of the way and take over, a long line of some powerful and dangerous people. Someone did this to get the guys out of the way. Do you think they would care about us? No. They would not. They would move us out of the way, or worse, kill us too," I said.

I had everyone's attention. They knew I was right. My phone rang. I answered it.

"Gina, its Alphe'. I just spoke with my brother. They sent him on an errand. Alcide had gone to pick up his lunch. He had not picked them back up. They were still meeting in the building. I'm sorry. I'm sure you knew when I was on the phone with him earlier, but I wanted to call you to confirm."

"Yes, I understand. Thank you for letting me know. I have already told the girls," I said.

I hung up the phone and all eyes were on me. I'm sure they were wondering what that conversation was about, if he had just confirmed their greatest fear, and hoping, he had not.

I took a deep breath. "Alphe' wanted to let us know that Alcide dropped them off earlier. He said he was sitting in the parking lot and the server had brought out a note. They sent him on an errand. He pick up his lunch while he was out. I can only assume that whoever did this sent him away to make sure there were no witnesses. He had not picked them back up yet. They were still in the building."

Everyone sat quietly for a moment. No one said a word.

After a few minutes, Carlita spoke up, "Wait! I have 'The Book'. It is in the safe in our room. I can go get it."

She jumped up and quickly left the room, as though she had to do it at that exact moment. She needed to do something.

I knew I had Sally's briefcase in the room as well. I went to get it. I brought it back and sat it on the dining table. Everyone eventually gravitated to it.

"He didn't take it because he must not have wanted me to think they were working today," I said, even though I knew exactly what he was doing.

Everyone gradually got up and followed suit. They went to their rooms, one by one. They wanted to see if anything was there that could help us. They brought anything they found to the table. Everyone put the 'Do Not Disturb' signs on their doors and did not talk to anyone on the way back to my room.

Carlita came back in with 'The Book.' Not the Holy Bible, but it was Drago's bible. The book contained everything on all business. It had all the financial info of every dollar paid in, by whom, and the amount still owed. It had names, dates, times, and places. It followed the money. Drago never traveled without it. He brought it on the trip and locked it in the safe the second he got there.

Antonella sat Marco's phone on the table. It was on the desk in their room. He must have forgotten it that morning. It had everyone's contact information in it, which would be helpful.

Everyone managed to find something that could be of use. I had to take control and not let anyone sit and think too much. We had to keep busy.

Our first item of business was to get new cell phones with the guy's numbers to replace theirs. We could say they were lost on the plane or in our luggage. We could make up some excuse as to why we need that many phones. Everyone on the outside needed to think they were still communicating with the guys, so when we called someone, their numbers show up.

"We are going to have to tell Alphe' our plan. He is going to have to help us," I announced.

"Can we trust him?" Antonella asked.

I knew we could. He got into some trouble when he was young, and Sally helped him. Sally had used him for years. If he trusted him, I knew we could too. He was not connected to any other families.

Everyone agreed.

Francesca asked, "What about Lil' Rocco? Did you forget about him? He was there, and we saw him leaving before the explosion. Do you think he knows the building blew up? He knows they were in there when he left."

Francesca was right about Lil' Rocco. I had not forgotten about him, not by a long shot. We needed to figure out his involvement in all of this before we did anything. If we could pull this off and everyone thought they were alive, then he would not know what happened. If he was involved, he had to be working with someone, because he did not have the guts to pull this off himself. He would lose all credibility.

"If he was responsible, then we can take care of Lil' Rocco ourselves, nephew or not," I said.

"Oh, so now you're gonna whack somebody? Who do you think you are? What are you, the Godfather? I mean the Godmother?" Adrianna asked, using her fingers to make air quotes as she said it with sarcasm.

"This is crazy," she said, riled up again.

I began to wonder if she was going to be a problem for me. I looked over at Francesca to handle it before I did.

Francesca got up, walked over to the bar, and back to Adrianna with a bottle of liquor. "Here, drink this. You need to calm down. We have an enemy out there who killed our husbands. Do you think it is a good idea to turn on each other? We have to work together. Now drink this and calm down. I don't want to have to tell you again."

She stood there holding a shot of whiskey in front of her.

Adrianna reached out, took the glass. In one big gulp, she drank it.

"You're right. I'm sorry," she said as she held out her empty glass for another shot.

It was a long night. Everyone stayed in my suite. There were a few catnaps here and there, but no real sleep. The sun was starting to creep in through the cracks in the drawn black out curtains and everyone was wide-awake, as if we had slept a full night. We were operating purely on adrenalin.

There was a light knock at the door. Francesca saw Alphe' through the peephole and opened the door.

He entered slowly with beignets and coffee. I could not help but think about our visit for beignets a few short days ago with our husbands. Life was quite different now.

Alphe' greeted everyone with a soft tone and red eyes. "Were you ladies able to get any more sleep than I did? I wanted to come check on you and see if I could help. I know you will need a ride to the police station and later to the airport. Have you made any arrangements yet?"

All eyes were on him, but no one answered. There was a silence and blank stares as he looked around the room.

"Have you spoken with the police yet?" He asked and looked again from person to person then back at me.

I finally spoke up, "No, and we are not going to."

He had a confused look on his face.

I stood up and walked over to him. "We need for everyone to believe the guys are still alive, at least for a while, and we need your help. Can we trust you? Our husbands certainly did. Will you help us?"

"Yes ma'am, of course, but why? And how are you going to pull that off?" he asked.

I told him, "We are working on a plan. You be here at six to pick us up for dinner, and we will explain more."

I also asked him to have his brother, Alcide, block off his schedule for the week, because we would need it to look like he is still driving the guys around as well. He agreed and went on his way.

We immediately went into planning mode. Adrianna started working on replacing the guy's cell phones. She explained we could just go to a local AT&T store, as she sat with her hand on her forehead holding it up as she was looking down.

In a voice almost as low as a whisper she said, "As long as we have phone numbers, we can just go get new phones, add them to our accounts, and get the phones immediately."

The plan immediately went into action.

We called Alphe' back to have him come back. We wanted the phones before our lunch. We were going to tell everyone the phones were lost in travel, except Marco's, and we were waiting on new ones. This would buy us a couple of days of no communication.

Adrianna finally looked up and said, "Let him take Marco's phone. They can download his contacts to the new phones, so we do not have to add them manually. Never mind, I cannot just sit here. I will go with him. I have to have something to do."

We had Adrianna change her clothes and put on a baseball cap so she could be inconspicuous.

"Good idea," I said, looking over at Carlita as if to say 'get her the hell out of here.'

Carlita understood and took charge. She called the phone store to get the phones ordered and paid for. Alphe' and Adrianna only had to get them programmed and pick them up. Adrianna grabbed Marco's phone, and they were off.

The more control I had, the better I felt. We were forming a plan.

The first step was the phones. The next step was to find out what Lil' Rocco's involvement was.

I immediately shared my strategy. "We are going to get dressed and go to lunch today. I'll invite Lil' Rocco to join us and include the guys in the number of people in the reservation. Once we are at the table, we can have Alphe' call the restaurant acting like Sally from the new cellphone to say their golf game is running late, and they won't make lunch. We will be able to see his reaction. Then, we will know."

I picked up the phone, dialed Lil' Rocco's number, took a deep breath, and looked around the room. All eyes were on me.

I heard his voice say, "Hello," on the other end of the line.

"Lil Roc, it's Aunt Gina. We're having lunch today at noon and wanted to invite you to join us."

I was certain he thought we were going to ask him where the guys were. Especially since, they did not come home last night, and we would ask for his help.

"Sure, Aunt Gina. It sounds great. See you soon." Lil' Rocco hung up his phone and immediately dials another number.

He told the person on the other end of the line that Gina had called him and invited him to lunch.

A deep voice on the other end asked, "What will you tell them?"

"I'll go back later and break the bad news to them. They will be devastated. They will ask me to take care of everything for them. Then we can do anything and everything we want. I will be in charge soon. I'll be in touch," Lil' Rocco said.

"I hope you're right, for your sake," the deep voice on the other end told Lil' Rocco before hanging up.

We had a few hours before lunch. We were able to take showers and freshen up. Sleep would have been great, but was not an option for any of us. We were focused on Lil' Rocco. We were ready to move on to step two of our plan.

7. SURPRISE

We arrived early so we could get a large table. We wanted to be settled before Lil' Rocco arrived.

Lil' Rocco walked into the restaurant and over to our table. We sat at the large table with place settings for eleven. I could see his wheels spinning as he tried not to show any surprise.

We had a moment of stillness as we stared at him.

Antonella finally spoke, "There he is."

He went around and kissed each one of us, but he never took his eyes off the empty chairs.

He winded his usual flattery of how beautiful we looked, as well as small talk. He asked us about our stay in New Orleans. It was nervous chatter.

"I understand congratulations are in order," Rocco said as he leaned around Adrianna from behind to kiss her on the cheek.

She nodded, smiled, and managed to muster up a thank you. She could handle that much at first sight of him.

I stepped in to bring the energy level up. I made excuses that we were tired from all of the partying.

I patted the table and said, "Come sit next to Aunt Gina, baby."

Everyone followed suit and started conversation. He finished his rounds and sat next to me. His eyes were still wondering around the table, as if counting the empty chairs.

Everyone was chitchatting as the waiter got drink orders. I told the waiter we were waiting on five more and asked him to give us a few more minutes. He nodded and walked away as we kept the conversation going.

I strategically placed my phone on the table, faced up, between me and Lil' Rocco. I wanted him to see the screen if it rang.

Lil' Rocco was curious and getting nervous. Our carefree demeanor made him uneasy. He was questioning in his mind of why we did not look upset, why we had not asked him for help, and why we were not demanding to know why our husbands did not come home last night.

However, he kept himself calm and tried to make small talk as he waited and wondered. Those five minutes must have seemed like an eternity to him. I doubt he even heard a word anyone said.

He could not take it anymore. "So, who are we waiting for?" he asked clearing his throat.

He did not ask if we were waiting on the guys or Uncle Sally. He asked as if he knew it could not be them and had to be someone else. No one answered him. There was an uncomfortable silence for about fifteen seconds until my phone rang. Perfect timing.

Adrianna had programmed Sally's photo to show when I received a call from him. Alphe' was outside with Sally's new phone.

I wanted to make sure Lil' Rocco saw Sally's name and photo appear when it rang. I was very slow to pick it up. His eyes immediately darted to my phone. I made a big deal about the call, as if I expected some sort of excuse for being late.

Ring, Ring.

I held the phone for the girls to see. Lil' Rocco was studying it closely, trying not to look too obvious.

I told everyone I was sure their golf game was running over, and they would stand us up for lunch.

"Golf? They are playing golf? Now?" Lil' Rocco said aloud, as if he could not control himself or his sudden outburst.

I answered the phone and tried to be animated. I smiled and nodded, confirming I was right. He was cancelling lunch.

Alphe', of course, was on the other end of the line.

I continued loudly, "I knew it. Well, at least we're being stood up for golf and not for work." I laughed. "Our dinner reservations are for seven so be back in time to clean up for dinner. Okay Sally? Have fun baby." I hung up the phone.

Lil' Rocco was obviously in shock. He took a big gulp of his drink, yelled for the waiter across the room, and motioned his hand in the air. He ordered a double whisky, straight up.

We had our answer. We were cutting eyes at each other around the table. We knew he was responsible, or at least partly. This proved he could not be trusted.

"So, um...," Lil' Rocco cleared his throat, "that was Uncle Sal on the phone?" he asked with a quiver to his voice.

I confirmed it was and made a joke that those rats were having fun without us. I looked him in the eyes.

Carlita started making plans. She told everyone we were going to have a great lunch on them and then go shopping to spend some of their money, while they were out playing.

Everyone laughed, except Lil' Rocco. His mind was reeling. His face was red, and he drank his entire drink in one shot.

The waiter came with ice buckets and two bottles of champagne. "Ladies... and sir, here are bottles of champagne ordered for you from...," he pulled his pad from his apron pocket and read, "from Sally and the guys. They said to enjoy lunch."

Lil' Rocco quickly grabbed his phone and jumped up. He stood up so quickly, he pushed his chair and it fell over. He acted as if he had an important issue come up.

"Ladies, I'm sorry, but I won't be able to stay for lunch either. I just had something come up. I had better handle it now. You know I need to be on my toes with the bosses in town. Sorry." He blew kisses and hurried out the door without the traditional Italian kisses goodbye or even a response from anyone, like the ones he made such a big deal to get upon his arrival.

The table was quiet. We ordered lunch and tried to eat. Having to act as though nothing was wrong was more difficult than expected.

I raised a glass to toast all of us and for a well-executed plan. Everyone raised their glasses and drank. That was all we could do. Our appetites were gone and would only be satisfied by Lil' Rocco paying for what he had done.

Carlita spoke after a few minutes and pointed out the obvious. "Now we know we can't trust him. He was a part of this. He killed our husbands. What now?"

8. PHASE I COMPLETE

Lil' Rocco left the restaurant as quickly as he could. We had Alcide outside waiting to follow him. We left the restaurant as well.

Alcide called Alphe' often to update us on Lil' Rocco's movements. It seemed he was driving around aimlessly. Alcide followed him for two hours. Lil' Rocco never noticed him.

We knew he was confused and scared. He had to wonder, did they get out in time? Were they suspicious of him all along? Did the building not blow up? Come to think of it, he had not heard anything on the news about an explosion. Did they know what he was up to? Why hadn't they contacted him? Are they going to kill him? He started to think that maybe they left immediately after he did, and maybe they did not know about the explosion. Maybe they would never know what he tried to do. Alcide said he looked like he did not know whether to call them or hide. He just drove around all afternoon. He drove while hitting the steering wheel and talked aloud to himself. Alcide could see him moving his arms around and shouting.

"What the hell was I thinking? They're going to kill me," he shouted to himself.

We arrived back at our hotel rooms by late afternoon. My plan was to call Lil' Rocco from Sally's phone. I was certain he would be afraid to pick up the phone, but I wanted to call anyway.

Alphe's phone rang just as we got into our suite. It was Alcide.

"He stopped. He finally calmed down and decided to stop due to sheer exhaustion," Alcide said.

We asked what he was doing. He said he was not doing anything. He was just sitting there. I guessed he did not know where to go.

Lil' Rocco was sitting in his car by the Lakefront. Alcide was watching him with binoculars. I thought it would be a good time to call him, since Alcide could see what his reaction would be.

I dialed his number with Sally's phone. Alcide saw Lil' Rocco jump when the phone rang. He slowly reached for his phone.

Still on the phone with Alphe', Alcide told us he was holding the phone, but had not looked at the screen to see who was calling. On the third ring, he finally looked and read *Uncle Sally*. He immediately threw the phone down on the seat and leaned into the steering wheel with his forehead on his hands shaking his head back and forth.

I hung up the phone on my end. "Just as I expected, he didn't answer, the little bastard." I could not help but throw the phone on the desk out of anger.

Phase one of our plan was complete. Lil' Rocco thought his plan failed, and they were still alive. Now, we had to fool the rest of the world.

Adrianna came to me and apologized. "I'm sorry Gina. I get it now. I understand what you're doing and why. I am sorry I questioned your motives. I will do whatever you need me to do. I'll even kill him." She smiled at me with her sad brown eyes. I knew she meant it and would kill him if I asked. I believe they all would do whatever I asked.

I reassured them that everything I was doing was for the good of all of us.

I decided we needed a change of scenery and needed to get away from Lil' Rocco. If we did not, I was going to kill him, and it definitely was not time for that. We needed more answers.

Everyone was looking to me for the next step.

Carlita chimed in, "How about Biloxi?"

I agreed, "Exactly what I was thinking. We leave in the morning."

Antonella sprang into action working with Alphe' to set it up. She had been pacing around the room and needed something to do. She started calling to make reservations at the Beau Rivage Casino and Resort.

I made the arrangements with Alphe' to clear his schedule so he could come with us to Biloxi. He would pick us up at nine the next morning to head to the Coast. We needed Alcide' to come with us to keep the charade going. We needed people we could trust. Alphe' and Alcide' had proven to be trustworthy.

Everyone was doing their part. Antonella was busy making hotel arrangements. Francesca was planning makeovers for us. Everyone needed to think everything was perfect. She thought this would help us feel better. She wanted us to look like a million bucks so it looked like we were being pampered by our husbands. Carlita was making dinner reservations, and Adrianna was helping each of them.

I sat back watching everything in motion and planning our next three chess moves. It was a process, but I was slowly getting everyone's buy in. They each managed to sneak in a quick smile here and there. We were starting to work together and needed to get into a groove if we were going to make this work.

We slept, not much, but better than before.

The alarm went off at seven, but we were already up and in action. We got packed and ready to leave New Orleans. Alphe' was downstairs waiting for us.

I stopped at the door and turned to the girls. "When we get on the highway and start heading east, we need to leave New Orleans behind us. I know it is easier said than done, but if we are going to fool anyone, we have to play the part. My mama always told me, just because you're feeling bad or sick or broke, it doesn't mean you have to run around looking like it!"

Everyone laughed.

"Let's take my mama's advice. Are we ready?"

Everyone nodded and were even a little excited. I think we were all ready to leave New Orleans. As much as we loved the city, it would always hold tragic memories for all of us.

Alphe' came to the door to help with bags and to get us safely to the car. Alcide would follow.

9. BILOXI BOUND

Biloxi 87 Miles, the sign read. There was silence in the car for a few minutes.

Finally, Antonella spoke, "Okay, enough. Gina is right. If we have any hopes of pulling this off, we need to stick together and put on our happy faces. I know it is difficult. Nevertheless, anyone who knows us will know something is wrong by looking at us. Let's face it, if they were still here, they would want us to do this. When we step out of this limo, we need to be our old selves."

"Hey, speak for yourself. We're not all old," Adrianna said jokingly to lighten the mood.

Everyone paused, and then started to laugh. I could not help but smile, as I looked up at her with a sigh of relief. I was not the only one who thought we could pull it off. I had everyone's buy in, even Adrianna.

Pop! All eyes turn to Carlita as she opened a bottle of champagne.

We knew from that moment, we needed to act like our fun-loving selves, no matter how we felt inside. Everyone smiled and grabbed a glass.

Adrianna asked what we were thinking, having champagne at nine in the morning. Carlita reached for the orange juice and gave her a pour.

She said, "Hello? Mimosas? With all this o.j., it's practically breakfast."

Alphe' was watching in the rearview mirror smiling. He could see us transforming.

We toasted to everything, to our husbands, to us, and to Alphe'.

"To the Godmothers," I said and winked at Adrianna. She smiled at me and put her head down in shame.

"Cheers to the Godmothers," everyone said and clinked their glasses.

"We need to come up with a special Godmother's drink to become our signature," Adrianna said.

As we got closer to Biloxi, everyone was confirming reservations and planning the next few days. The realization of what we were trying to pull off hit me again. Different emotions took over. I had to put on my game face. The most important thing I learned from my husband was never to show fear or weakness. He would always say, the minute you do, someone is waiting in the wings to take you out and take control. I could hear his voice in my head. I knew if we had any chance of executing this plan and having anyone listen to me, I had to be in full control and look as though I belonged in this position.

"Now, when we get there, it's on." They looked at me to see if I had anything else to say. I was not sure if I said that more for their benefit, or mine.

"Only one mile to go," Alphe' informed us through the window between the front and back of the car.

We saw the casino on the left and the Gulf water glistening as we took the ramp over the water.

The sand was sugar white and inviting. Looking out over the Gulf made it hard to believe anything was wrong. It was beautiful. The car slowly pulled into valet.

The bellman said as he approached the car and opened our doors, "Welcome to the Beaux Rivage. Checking in today?"

Alphe' took the lead. He assisted and shielded us from having to speak to anyone.

We decided to talk about the guys and mention their names every chance we got. We could not be too careful and did not know who might be listening.

As the bellman placed our luggage on a cart and led us into the lobby, Alphe' asked him if the guys had checked in yet. He was not sure, so he brought us to registration to ask the front desk clerk. Alphe' asked if they had arrived yet.

"No Sir, they haven't arrived yet, but the reservation shows they called ahead and made some special arrangements for their wives. You are lucky ladies. Your husbands must really love ya'll. They have arranged an entire day of beauty and relaxation for you to enjoy today. We will get you checked into your suites, and we will take care of your luggage. You just follow Angelo, the handsome Italian behind you, and he will take you to the Bellisimo Spa to start your day. Do not worry about a thing. We will take it from here," she said.

I arranged for Alphe' and Alcide to have rooms at the hotel as well. I wanted them to be close by if we needed them. Alphe' knew our schedule so he could check in on us.

Angelo has jet black, thick hair that he slicked back. His eyes were a beautiful green. He had dimples that melted you when he smiled.

Angelo stood behind us smiling. He nodded and said hello as we turned to greet him.

"Good morning ladies. I'm Angelo. Follow me. I will take your luggage up to your suites later. You ladies are going straight to the Bellisimo Spa. Your husbands called me personally this morning to make sure you are treated like royalty."

We all looked at each other with slight smiles thinking, 'so far so good.'

Angelo sat us in a beautiful and tranquil relaxation room. He excused himself and said he would be right back. The mood in the room changed immediately, as he walked away. Each of us sat quietly. We were mentally exhausted from trying to keep up the act.

Angelo walked in with another young and equally handsome man. He introduced him as Giovanni, Gio for short. He explained how we would spend the day.

He gave each of us a locker key. In each of the lockers were workout clothes, swimsuits, and robes, compliments of our husbands.

First, we were going to start with a great workout, a swim, a dip in the hot tub, and a massage. After our massages, we were going to shower. Then, we would go to the salon for makeovers.

As always, Antonella lightened the mood. "You forgot the most important thing. Lunch!"

"No, we didn't forget. You'll have a light lunch after your massages," said Angelo.

"Light?" she asked. "I hope you don't mean diet."

The handsome duo laughed, assured her we would enjoy our lunches, and left.

We went to our lockers and opened them, as if we did not know what was inside. We took out the workout clothes first and went into the changing rooms. Each of us went into the workout area one at a time, as we finished dressing.

Antonella was the last to enter the workout room. Angelo walked over to her and reached out his hand to her to bring her over to the rest of us.

"What's next?" she asked.

Angelo smiled and said, "Let's get through the workout first. Then, we can focus on what's next."

"Workout?" she asked and looked up at him. "I thought that was the workout. I broke a sweat jumping up and down, stretching and bending, just to get into this outfit! You mean there's more?"

Everyone laughed.

"You're going to be trouble, aren't you," Gio chimed in.

"You don't know the half of it," Francesca said and shook her head.

There was music playing and the workout was not bad. I think they took it easy on us for our first time. It was nice to focus on the workout and music. The more intense it was, the better I felt. It was as if I was stronger with every movement.

Next, we got in our swimsuits and met Angelo and Gio at the pool. Antonella came out last with a robe over her swimsuit. She walked over to the men, backed up to them, and looked over her shoulder.

"You've been waiting to see me in my bikini all morning haven't you?" she flirted.

They both grinned and nodded, with an affirming yes.

"Well no funny business, I'm a married woman," she said.

We looked at her. She realized what she said. Trying not to react, we all jumped in the pool, everyone except Antonella. She knew after her comment, she would have to lighten the mood. She stood by the side of the pool with her robe closed tightly, holding the sashes in her hands.

"Is everything okay?" Angelo asked.

She responded jokingly, "After you. Don't think you're getting a free look at this bod!"

Angelo and Gio laughed. They took their shirts off and jumped in the pool. Of course, she was not wearing a bikini. She wore a whole piece with a skirt attached. She called it her bikini just the same.

As always, Antonella entertained by hitting a few poses before jumping in.

We spent thirty minutes doing water aerobics. The time flew by. We were cutting up and trying to stay above water without drowning. It was a nice distraction.

"Now we can get in the hot tub to loosen up those muscles for your massages," Gio said.

"It is co-ed?" Antonella jokingly asked.

"Come on trouble. You're sitting by me!" Gio told her with a smile.

The hot tub was in the relaxation room. This is where they would leave us to have lunch. There was a table in the middle of the room with flowers and five place settings. It was not there the first time we came in the room. They had it brought in especially for us.

We reserved the spa for the time we were in there. No one would be allowed in. No one knew we were there, but we wanted to be safe, just in case.

The relaxation area was beautiful. It had a huge hot tub, a warm dip tub, and a cold dip tub. The hot tub was huge with a waterfall on the back wall you could stand under. It was amazing. The room was all shades of blue and had a different mosaic behind each tub. The ceiling was a very light shade of blue and the glare of the water was glistening on it. A slatted wall separated the tubs from a couple of rows of stone, heated chaise lounge chairs. They overlooked the Gulf. Soft spa music was playing. A server walked in with a cart as Angelo and Gio were leaving.

The cart had a beautiful crystal bowl containing cut fruit. There were Shrimp Louis salads with remoulade dressing. Lemon water was iced in a decanter. Champagne chilling in an ice bucket.

The food, music, and atmosphere was truly spectacular. I do not think any of us wanted to leave those four walls. We relaxed and enjoy it. Gio came in to let us know our therapists would be in to get us shortly.

Each of us went back to our respective massage rooms. The massages were exactly what we needed. The rooms smelled of eucalyptus and were dimly lit. Candles burned for the right amount of light. Soft music was playing. The room temperature and the warm blankets were perfect. There was no acting, no having to smile or be happy, just quiet. We could have one hour to be alone with our thoughts. I had to plan our next move, or two. Sally always said most people were a chess move ahead. He had to be three or four.

The massage therapist asked how the massage was and I replied softly. I sat up and walked slowly to the relaxation room where I would wait for everyone else.

The girls started to come back to the room in their white, fluffy robes, yawning and stretching as they sat down on the heated chaise lounges.

The door opened. Angelo and Gio were back to take us to our next adventure for the day.

I was beginning to feel more powerful with each passing moment. Everyone looked to me for guidance. I was completely in charge and settling into our new reality. I was mentally ready for what was ahead. I realized the workouts would helped me to feel physically strong, but had to work on the mental aspect of the game.

Angelo and Gio told us that there was one more phase to our pampering day.

As wonderful as the day was, we could not be too wrapped up in relaxation and enjoyment.

10. MAKE ME OVER

Angelo and Gio brought us to the salon. The final step was a makeover. They brought us to the Beau Belle Salon. Each of us picked a chair and sat down. We continued to act as if everything was a surprise, even though we made the arrangements. It was nice pampering ourselves. Sally was never the romantic or spontaneous type. I could do whatever I wanted, but he never surprised me with gifts, or anything like this. None of the guys was, except maybe Luigi. Of course, he was not married.

Angelo told the stylist, "Okay now, ya'll have fun and we will be back to get you at six. Watch out for this one, she's trouble." He nodded his head at Antonella and put his hands on her shoulders.

The stylist asked each of us what service we would like. No one answered. Even though we knew we made the appointments, we had not thought what changes we wanted, if any.

I finally spoke up, "I want something totally different. Change the color and cut it. Do whatever you want."

All eyes turn to look at me.

"Me too, make me glamorous," Carlita said.

"Me too," each chimed in.

The stylists were excited. They never were able to do what they wanted.

"This is going to be fun," one said.

The stylists walked to the back to get color and other supplies.

"Okay, we're going to take before and after photos. These makeovers are going to be badass," one of them said.

"We are all about badass these days," I said as I followed her to the back.

"Okay ladies, let's head over to the shampoo bowls and get this party started," she said as she cranked up the music and walked us over to the chairs in the back.

The salon was very different from the spa area. It was well lit, had upbeat music playing, and full of energy. Each of us took a chair and leaned back. We enjoyed the head massages and the fun idle conversations between the stylists.

They went back and forth with each other, challenging the other to see which will be the biggest transformation. We were up for the contest and started having fun with it too. They whispered to us while picking our color and style, so the others could not hear us.

Color started going on and foil highlights too. When each head towel came off, the stylists giggled louder. Red, black, brown, and blonde were chosen. The scissors began snipping, and we were all glancing at each other optimistically.

This was exactly what we needed, a brand-new us. With our new hairdos, we walked over to the next area of the salon to see the nail techs and makeup artists. We took turns with each service and felt a little better about what we were doing. The changes seemed appropriate for the new lives we were starting.

Antonella said, "Our husbands would be proud of us," as she was admiring herself in the mirror.

We walked back to the relaxation area to get dressed.

Carlita said, "Oh no. These clothes will not do. If we are going to rock these new looks, we need new clothes and attitudes to match," as she was standing at the three way mirror.

"Badass, remember," she pointed out as she grabbed both corners of the old shirt she had on. "I feel frumpy. This is not badass. It's just bad."

Adrianna told everyone to wait and not to get dressed. She walked into the spa, got one of the stylists, and asked them to call the boutique to let them know we were on our way. We wanted all new clothes.

Adrianna and the stylist came back in. The stylist said, "Follow me. The boutique just closed, but they are going to open it up to you for a private shopping experience. I will bring you down the hall to them and let Angelo and Gio know to pick you ladies up down there in an hour or so. We will get our after pictures then. I'll come down in an hour with the camera."

Everyone left the puffy white spa robes on to go shopping. Our existing clothes were not worthy of our new looks. The stylists put our hair back in towels so they could fix it after we were dressed in our new duds. They wanted the after makeover photos to be perfect.

11. BEAU CHIC APPAREL

The sales women welcomed us and were very nice to have re-opened the store for our little shopping spree.

One of them said warmly, "Welcome ladies. I hear you've had a day of beauty and now you need the clothes to match?"

"Yes. We want to leave here, new women. So, crank the music back up. Girls, lets hide our crazy and find us some new giddy ups," Adrianna said.

As soon as the radio came on, a Miranda Lambert and Carrie Underwood song played called *Something Bad*.

"OOOHHH something bad about to happen," we all sang.

∞100∞

We tried on clothes for over an hour. We were finally having fun. Everything clicked. The rest of the girls finally understood. This is what we had to do, and the guys would want it for us.

Carlita threw the curtain of the dressing room open. She had on a short, sequined skirt. She never wore anything flashy, especially all sequins, or short, or skirts for that matter.

"Damn, look at those legs!" Adrianna yelled.

All eyes turned to her, instead of Carlita. Everyone wanted to see why she was yelling.

"Well seriously, with those maw-maw clothes she wears, who knew that was under there," Adrianna continued laughing.

Adrianna jumped up, ran over to Carlita, and walked her over to the three-way mirror. It had a step up and a small runway platform that looked like a small stage.

"Look at you. You are hot. Now, put these on," Adrianna said as she handed her a pair of high-heeled Christian Louboutin shoes.

She also chose her a pair from a new designer, Lindy B. Of course, with all of the new clothes, we had to get new shoes and bags too.

Carlita stood there looking at herself in the mirrors. She always hid her figure in dowdy, conservative clothing.

Francesca stood next to Carlita. "Do you have this skirt in my size?" she joked.

Everyone hurried to the shoe section. We tried on nearly everything in the store. Hangers were everywhere and shoeboxes were stacked on top of each other. Each of us had our own piles. It was the quickest hour of my life. However, it was not the cheapest.

The sales girl walked over to us. "So ladies, have we made any decisions?"

I slapped one hand down on the large stack of clothes and the other on a larger stack of shoes and said, "We're getting ready to make a lot of big decisions. I'll take it all!"

The girls looked at me and laughed. They knew exactly what I meant. They slapped their hands down on their piles too. The sales girls looked at each other in shock. We had just made their sales quotas for the year.

They started ringing up the piles.

"Not this one, I'm wearing it out of here and these too," Antonella said as she pointed to a pair of high heels.

Everyone else immediately turned to their stacks and followed her lead.

Carlita kept on her short sequined skirt and new Lindy B shoes. She was ready to go.

"You'll have to ring me up like this," she said as she jumped up to sit on the counter so the sales girl could scan the tag on the blouse she was wearing.

I asked them to charge everything to our rooms and send them up later.

There was a knock at the door of the shop. It was Angelo and Gio coming to get us. I asked the sales girl to let them know we would meet them in the lobby in thirty minutes. The stylist came back with the camera to take our *after* photos.

Adrianna texted Alphe' to ask him to meet us in the lobby, so he could take us to dinner.

Everyone posed in their new outfits on the runway. We looked like Charlie's Angels plus two.

"Not bad for five middle-aged women," Antonella said.

"Middle-aged? How many one hundred year olds do you know?" I asked.

"Well, maybe our boobs are not where they used to be, and we have corns on our toes. And maybe our backs and knees hurt occasionally. And maybe we do pee a little every time we laugh, but I still think we look hot," Francesca said.

"Absolutely," we all agreed.

12. SUPERMODELS

Each of us walked out of the boutique a new woman. We were standing upright with confidence and smiles. It was a re-awakening for all of us. We needed it in order to proceed with this plan, this farce, and this elaborate plot to fool everyone we knew. It was time to let everyone see the new us with our new looks and new attitudes. We made our way to the casino lobby.

The casino and hotel were beautiful. The décor was elegant. It was gold and black with exquisite floor mosaics, blown glass chandeliers, and extraordinary artwork. It smelled incredible. They pumped fragrance throughout the entire property.

The elevator door opened, we walked out, and crossed the lobby side by side. We did not hide any of us. We felt like supermodels walking toward Angelo, Gio, and Alphe'. Supermodels who were walking in slow motion with our hair blowing back in the wind and music playing, you cannot forget the music. Jaws dropped as we approach the guys.

Antonella stopped, threw out a leg, posed, and asked, "You boys looking for some hot dates?"

They just stood and looked at us.

"Wow! Ya'll look incredible, I mean really great, sensational!" Gio said as he looked at each of us.

I could not help but watch Angelo's reaction. He winked at me and walked over to Antonella.

"Oh yeah baby, really hot," he said as he leaned into Antonella.

He held out his arm for her to take and then turned to me to take the other. We did not mind. He was gorgeous.

"Well Alphe', what do you think? You have not uttered a word. Are you in shock?" Carlita asked him.

Alphe' was always a gentleman. It was his southern upbringing.

After a pause and a long look back at Carlita, "Ladies, I thought ya'll looked great before, but now, I mean, triumph! Ya'll are knockouts!"

We all smiled back at him. We knew how well we looked. He held out his hand to Carlita waiting for her to reach back for his.

As we walked to the car, he told us he had spoken with our husbands and was supposed to bring us to the restaurant to meet them.

Everyone turned to him immediately. That statement snapped us out of the high we were on and back to reality. He hated to do it, but he had to keep us focused. We understood, but we felt so good that we did not want to get back to reality so quickly.

Angelo and Gio kept saying how our husbands were going to go crazy when they saw their hot wives. We just made jokes and agreed with them, to keep it going.

We had the back room of Hugo's reserved for the night. Hugo's was an old Italian restaurant in Biloxi. Sally loved it. They were famous for their pizza. When Sally would go to New Orleans as a kid to see his grandmother, they would drive to the Coast often, sometimes just for a pizza and a drive down the beach. Every time he mentioned it, he would always describe it to me: how it looked, how it smelled, and what fond memories he had of it.

As we walked through the main restaurant, I could hear his voice describing everything I was seeing. He said it had red and white checkered table clothes and red candles with those little nets. There was a half wall between the bar and the tables, which had lighted Budweiser lights every three feet, kind of like a big snow globe. Inside the light were moving Clydesdale horses. The lighting was dim. There were red leather booths with leather on the walls. It was exactly as Sally described.

I loved everything about it. I loved the look, I loved the smell, and I loved hearing his voice in my head describing it. I do not think anything had changed over the years.

We ordered our dinner and ordered too much. It looked like the guys were with us. We laughed at the amount of food, fattening food at that, laid out on the table.

"Boy, we would be in big trouble if Angelo and Gio saw us eating this pizza," Francesca said.

The desserts started coming after the meal. It was hard for us to resist the Italian heavenly desserts. Well, hard for everyone except Adrianna. She cut a piece, if you could call it that, of the Italian crème cake. We could not help but make fun of her. She would have more cake on her plate if she knocked the crumbs off the knife. Francesca cut a piece next. It was a small slab.

"Now, this is how you cut a piece of cake. You should be ashamed to dirty a plate for what you have," she said showing Adrianna her plate.

"Angelo and Gio would approve of my slice," Adrianna countered as she smiled.

Neely ran the Biloxi organization. He had always been my favorite of all the other guys. He was loyal and did what he could for the family. He manage to always do good things for the community. Everyone liked him and so did I. I hoped he had not crossed over and was helping Lil' Rocco. So far, we found no evidence to prove he had any part in Lil' Rocco's plan.

We called Neely and had him set everything up, but told him we wanted a romantic dinner with our husbands. Business would not be the topic of conversation, and he was not invited. We had him pre-order the food and included our husband's favorites. We had dinner and discussed the next steps. The plan would need to move along, because these excuses would not work forever.

We planned the next few days. We booked a day of golf for the guys for the next morning and made lunch reservations in their names through the hotel. From there on out, we had to assume the little bastard Rocco had his spies in the hotel and around town. We also ordered show tickets for ten.

Adrianna had the idea to spend the day out at the pool. She was in charge of making plans for our day. She ordered flowers, champagne, and lunch to be sent out to us from our husbands. We needed noticing, as if nothing was wrong in our world.

As we continued, I blurted out, "It's a shame it took something like this to make our husbands so generous."

I looked up realizing what I said and that I did so out loud. All eyes were on me. No one laughed. Carlita broke the silence to take attention away from me.

"Golf, okay," she asked quickly. "What next?"

I sat back for a minute to get myself in check.

Francesca also stepped in to keep the ideas rolling.

We had a lot to do. Next, we had to schedule a private poker game for them. That was something they would do if they were here and it was easy to schedule a private room so no one else was allowed in. That would buy us an entire night.

Carlita also stated the obvious. We needed to find a way to contact Lil' Rocco and get him to Biloxi. I had to re-engage. She was right, but it was not the next step in my plan.

I spoke up, "First we need to try to have the weekly call to see what's going on. We need to make sure that no one suspects anything. We are still safe because no one knows where we are. Let's see if Angelo and Gio can help us. We only need an office with a speakerphone. We will have to figure out how to say just enough so they think the guys are on the phone."

Easier said than done. I had the plan, but execution was going to be the challenge.

"Any ideas? I asked.

Adrianna had an idea. She explained, "I have several saved voicemails from Luigi on my cell I think we can use."

She sent Alphe' to get a handful of small recording devices so we could record all of our husbands voicemails, which contained each of their voices.

"We can try to extract anything that could possibly be useful in the messages. Maybe we will have enough to pull off a short call," Adrianna said.

Everyone was intrigued and supported her idea, since she had the most knowledge about technology and cellphones. It was the only idea any of us had.

We started to listen to all of our messages and then turned in to get some well-needed sleep.

13. FOOLED BY THE POOL

Each of us had an early breakfast for two delivered. We also put some of our husband's laundry in a bag to send out for cleaning. We slipped on our new swimsuits and met by the pool. We tried to think of every little detail of what our days would be like if they were with us, what they would eat, what they would wear, and so on.

A pool attendant greeted us. "Ladies, could you please follow me? Your husbands called from the golf course and set up a private pool cabana. And in a bit, I'll serve you lunch."

The pool cabanas were elegant. The awnings were black and white with gold fringe. They had long striped panels hanging to the ground and tied back with big gold tassels. The tables were iron and glass. The chairs and chaise lounges were lush and comfortable with beautiful turquoise throw pillows and towels. A beautiful flower arrangement and two bottles of champagne chilling complimented the center of the tables.

Angelo came to the pool to check on us a few times. He kneeled down on the side of my chaise lounge chair and put his arm on the arm of my chair.

He asked, "So, when do I get to meet this husband of yours? I'm starting to wonder if he really exists."

I know I had a stunned look on my face. I had to do something to change the subject.

"Why? Would you rather spend time with him than me?" I jokingly asked.

I was flirting with him. I had not flirted in twenty-five years. My mind was reeling, my heart was racing, and my face had to be red. The three R's, that is bad. Was I flirting, or did this gorgeous man half my age think I was senile?

"Absolutely not. I'll spend as much time with you as you'll let me," he responded as he got up.

Wow. He was flirting back, or at least I think he was. Hell, I do not know. Did he feel sorry for me because I was flirting? Man, could he turn it on when he wanted to. He stood up and leaned down over me.

"As much time as you want," he whispered.

He brushed his hand across my arm as he was walking away. I was not imagining this. I had to sit back a minute to think.

He was flirting, that was not my imagination. He repeated himself, in case I missed it. Maybe he thought I was hard of hearing. Could I even go there? I just sat there quietly.

Gio walked over with the waiter. Lunch was ready. Angelo walked over to see what foods we ordered. He saw salads and fruit. He complimented us on our good choices.

"Okay ladies, enjoy the day. We will see ya'll at three to work out," he said with a winked as he was leaving.

He was looking directly at me, but I'm sure all of the girls believed it was for them.

A group of women was nearby in the sun. They were not in a cabana. One of them walked over to the cabana, threw the curtain open, and walked in. She put her hands on her hips.

Smiling, she said, "Okay, so who do we need to kill to get a cabana like this?"

Stunned, Carlita asked, "Excuse me?"

The stranger laughed and explained herself. She said everyone at the pool was trying to figure out who we were and how we got so lucky to get a cabana. They were hard to get. They tried to get one every day, but were still out there baking in the heat.

"We figured you must have bribed or killed someone to get it with all of this first class treatment you've been getting," she said and laughed.

Realizing she was teasing, Francesca said, "Well, if we told you that, we would have to kill you too." She continued with a smile, "Our husbands did all of this for us."

The woman left the cabana. We could hear her telling her friends how we landed it. She told them they needed to send their husbands to learn from ours.

We rolled our eyes at each other. She was loud and obnoxious. She did call a little attention to us though, and that was one of our goals.

All afternoon people passed by and commented on the generosity of our husbands. Surely, Lil' Rocco had to be hearing this. He had to have spies. We knew he was probably looking for us in New Orleans by now. I was certain he called the hotel and knew we checked out. Basic deduction would tell him we were in Biloxi. I would assume so anyways. Maybe, I was giving him too much credit. If so, he would be looking for us. It came with the territory.

After our day at the pool, we went to the gym for our workout with Angelo and Gio.

The girls asked me what had gotten in to me; if I was trying to make them look bad and who I was trying to impress. They watched my every move. I kept telling them I was not trying to impress anyone. I was not sure I believed that.

Finally, Angelo spoke, "I'm impressed," he said to the group.

"Me too," Gio chimed in.

It was as if I was trying for the Olympics. I did not want to look out of shape, old, or especially weak. It was the best workout I ever had in my life. I could have a heart attack, but it would have been well worth it.

After the workout, we went back to our rooms to clean up. Then, the girls came to my suite. There was a knock at my door. I walked over in slow motion. I felt that Ironman workout in parts of my body I did not know could hurt.

Leaning against the door was Francesca. "Let's just order in tonight," she said without even looking up.

Antonella was already a step ahead. She was going to order for ten, but Carlita stopped her. She told her to say the guys had a dinner meeting out and to order only for us.

"We can't possibly keep eating for two every meal and look like supermodels!" she said and everyone agreed.

Once everyone was at the table in my room, I put my phone in the middle of the table. We had a lot of work to do.

I had two undeleted voicemails from Sally on my phone. I pressed play for us to hear. Each girl followed.

Antonella had seven. She never deleted anything until her phone warned her that her voicemail was nearly full.

"You never can tell when you'll need an old voicemail," she said. It definitely worked to our advantage this time.

Carlita, Francesca, and Adrianna only had one each.

I had to turn the floor over to Adrianna. This was her project. She took the lead.

She had Alphe' get as many recording devices as Best Buy had. He dropped them off while we were at the pool. She also had a pack of sticky notes and pens laid out in the center of the table. She explained her idea.

"We're going to record certain responses from these voicemails and use them on the call. Let's see what we've got," she said excitedly.

We listened to all of the messages again and made notes of the contents on each of them. She would record certain parts of each voicemail on the recording device.

Carlita pressed play on her voicemail and heard Nico's voice, "Hey babe. I talked to the grandkids this morning and told them that we made it to New Orleans. And yes, we will bring them something back. We will see you this evening for dinner. Hope you guys are having fun today. Love you."

Her eyes filled with tears, but she wiped them away quickly, as not to get lost in the emotion.

Adrianna had the best and longest voicemail. Luigi was always butt dialing everyone. He did this a few weeks ago to her, and she did not answer. It went to her voicemail.

She did not pay any mind to it when she realized it was not a message for her. It was a couple minutes of him talking to the other guys. We listened to it multiple times and very carefully. We were able to get several good recordings from it.

We played it again, "You guys better get your act together. Things ain't looking good. Lil' Rocco set up a call for tomorrow with everyone at 2:00. "

She clicked it off. We could use that one to get Lil' Rocco to the hotel. That was going to be a very valuable recording.

Once we heard everything, I knew we had enough to pull off a short call. We set it up for the next day. This would be the test to see if we could do this or not. If we could pull off a call, we certainly could do what we had planned.

We called Lil' Rocco. He did not answer. It went to voicemail. We hung up and texted him. I think he was still afraid to answer. We needed to get him to the hotel to find out why he killed our husbands and if he was working alone.

We spent hours perfecting the recordings. We wrote on a sticky note exactly what was on each device. This helped us keep them straight.

There were ten in all. We were going to have to be creative.

Sticky note #1: *Hey.*

Sticky note #2: *You guys better get your act together, things ain't looking too good.*

Sticky note #3: *Okay*

Sticky note #4: *Maybe somebody needs to just disappear.*

Sticky note #5: *My wife's got more balls than you.*

Sticky note #6: *One day you might make all the decisions, but it ain't today.*

Sticky note #7: *I said no.*

Sticky note #8: *You do what I'm telling you.*

Sticky note #9: *Joke; You know why Italians are considered magicians? We can make people disappear. Capishe?*

Sticky note #10: *Just making sure you heard me.*

Once we listened to everything and made recordings, we knew what we had to work with. We had to be careful to make it work.

We were ready to test it.

"Well, is everyone ready to get this done and see how we do?" I asked in my deep Sally voice.

All eyes looked around the room. They were looking for Sally.

"Oh my God, you sound just like him. It is earie. You gave me chills," Adrianna said rubbing the cold chills on her arms.

Everyone laughed.

When you are together as long as we were, it happens. They say you start looking alike too. Thank goodness, we had not gotten to that point. He was a little rounder than I wanted to be. Sometimes I would talk to Sally in his own voice. It drove him crazy how much I sounded like him. If he had a bad day and took it out on me, I would give it right back to him in his own voice. Usually, he would stop when he realized what he was doing.

Sometimes it would make him grouchy, and sometimes he would smile and say, "I'm sorry baby. I don't mean to take it out on you."

Most of time I was just being playful, but it certainly was a talent that would come in handy in the future.

14. HIT REWIND

Angelo and Gio came through for us. They were kind enough to let us use their office for our call. Everyone was sitting at a round, conference table in the fitness center office. It was out of the way located behind the fitness center. We had complete privacy.

Carlita dialed the number and hushed everyone. After a few seconds, we could hear the phone click on the other end as everyone was joining the call.

Lil' Rocco was first on the call, "Hello, we're all here Boss."

We each had a job. I was in charge of the phone mute button. If something went wrong, I could control the damage. Everyone else had recorders.

"Press play, press play," I whispered and pointed to the word *HEY* written on a sticky note next to one of the recorders, which was in front of Carlita.

"Hey," played loudly in Nico's voice from the recorder. It startled us. I immediately gave the thumbs down to lower the volume.

I pointed to Adrianna, mouthed the word *play* and unmuted the phone.

"You guys better get your act together. Things ain't looking too good," played in Luigi's voice.

There was silence over the phone. We were all shrugging our shoulders and did not know what to say next. No one on the other end wanted to step out on a limb and speak first. They did not know to whom Luigi was referring. We hoped someone would speak up, anyone. We especially hoped the guilty party would speak up, and he did.

Lil' Rocco spoke after what seemed like five minutes of silence, but it was actually a few seconds.

"Boss, I know things ain't great, but it's going to get better real soon. Maybe I should drive over. Where are ya'll? Biloxi? I assume you left New Orleans. I called the hotel when I could not reach you on your cells. They said you checked out. We can sit down this week to talk about it. I will come to wherever you are," Lil' Rocco said.

We had not thought about the hotel. We should have stayed checked in. Everyone looked around the table and shrugged. We missed that one.

I looked at Carlita and signaled her to press play.

"You guys better get your act together, things ain't looking too good," repeated the recorder.

I slapped the table twice, shook my head, and pointed to #4 while holding up four fingers with my other hand. I then rolled my eyes and put my face in my hands on the table.

Before she could press play, Lil' Rocco spoke up again, "Boss, we heard you. I really think it is going to get better. Can I come over to see you? I had to make some changes this month, but I think they will be for the better. You'll see."

I hit mute and everyone was reading the sticky notes, trying to listen to the conversation, and talk amongst ourselves, all at the same time.

I reached over and hit play on the recorder in front of Antonella. "One day you might make all the decisions. It ain't today".

No one responded. I then realized the phone was still on mute.

"Shit, hurry rewind it and play it again".

Antonella played #4 again. "Maybe someone just needs to disappear.

Carlita immediately clicked play next to sticky note #8. "You do what I'm tellin' you," played in Sally's voice.

Carlita pointed to Antonella and she pressed play. "Okay," played in Nico's voice.

Lil Rocco said, "Okay Boss. I will come tomorrow. I will be there at 1:00. Biloxi?"

I motioned for Antonella to hit Nico's "okay" again, but it would not rewind. She kept trying.

"Boss, is that okay?" Lil' Rocco repeated himself.

I had to do something, anything, or we were done.

Before I could stop myself, I said, "Okay Roc," channeling my innermost Sally.

All eyes turned to me in shock. I had to admit it was a little unsettling for me as well.

Carlita clicked the phone to hang up, before anyone asked anything else. Everyone's head dropped to the table. They each looked up at me and started laughing.

"Okay, so that was a train wreck. If we can get through that, we can get through anything. I feel like I just ran a marathon. Good job Adrianna. Your plan worked. Now what?" Antonella asked, looking around the table.

Well, the obvious question was now that we had Lil' Rocco coming to us, what do we do with him when we get him here? It was time to figure out why he did it and if he acted alone. We had to think the next phase through carefully. This was not going to be as easy as pressing buttons or disconnecting a call if needed. Even if we could get him to tell us everything, what would we do with him after he told us? We could not let him go; because he would know we knew the guys were gone. He would tell everyone and work to get rid of us.

Everyone looked at each other in silence, afraid of the answer. However, we all knew the answer to the question.

"Oh, trust me. I have a few ideas. And no, we are not going to kill him... yet. Carlita, get a pen. Here is what we are going to need. Get Alphe'. He said he has family in Biloxi, or close by. We need a secluded place. It needs to be somewhere we can keep him, and no one will ask questions. We also need to make a list of things we need from Walmart and a beauty supply store," I instructed.

Antonella asked, "What could we possibly need from a beauty supply store. Are we going to give Rocco a makeover too?"

"Something like that. Let's just say he's going to get in touch with his feminine side," I said with an evil smirk on my face. "Carlita, are you ready for my list?"

Carlita answered, "Go."

I ticked off the list to Carlita. "A large crock-pot for hot wax and wax of course, plenty of waxing strips, Kotex, and make them extra-large. If they still make the belts for them, get them too. Let's do tampons, alcohol, clothespins, razor blades, a curling iron, medical tape, and scissors. That should get us started. If anyone has any other suggestions, chime in any time."

The girls made jokes and asked if we were going to scare him into talking with nail polish and hair spray or if we were going to paint his toes and curl his hair.

I could not resist making a joke at his expense, as well. "Well, it will be a hair raising experience for him."

The light bulbs went off in their heads. They finally got where I was heading and laughed.

Francesca said, "Oh this is going to be fun," as she rubbed both hands together in excitement.

We got Alphe' started on all of the things we needed. We called him to the room to give him our list of supplies. Alphe' reached out for the list and began to laugh.

"Uh ladies, I believe you gave me the wrong list. There is nothing but girly stuff on here," he said as he reached out to hand the list back to Carlita with his cheeks slightly blushing.

"No, you have the correct list. Are you macho enough to go shopping for those items?" she asked as she gave him back the list.

"I guess I'm comfortable enough in my own skin to do this. I believe a man needs to get in touch with his feminine side every now and then. But what on earth could you possibly be planning with all of this?" he asked as he looked around at each of us. "Well, I guess the less I know the better. Right?" He took the list and headed out.

We all chuckled after he left. Imagining the experience he was going to have while trying to figure out what some of the items were was comical. I would have loved to be a fly on the wall to watch him look for everything.

We went back to our rooms and got ready for dinner.

15. SHE'S THE MAN

We stayed close to the casino and hotel for dinner. There was a great Italian restaurant in the casino. We had reservations for an early dinner and thought we could gamble a little to clear our minds to get ready for the next day. We were not card players like the guys. We played slots for fun.

We went to our respective suites and picked out one of our new outfits. We planned to meet back at my suite at six so we could all walk down together. I thought it was better for us to stick together; strength in numbers was a good rule to follow.

As we were walking through the lobby to the bar, I could not help but look around. I had a feeling we were being watched. I did not want it to be obvious, but I needed to know.

"Let's take a look in the jewelry store towards the entrance," I said as I steered everyone.

Antonella said, "Don't forget our reservation time."

"The guys will be there to hold the table for us," I said loudly and looked back at them.

They knew I had reason to say that and followed me into the store.

I leaned down to look in one of the cases and called Carlita over to show her something. She leaned close down by me.

I whispered, "I think I just saw Lil' Rocco. He is following us. He must have been here today and acted like he was not coming until tomorrow. He maybe on to us. We need to let everyone know and head to the restaurant. I will browse near Francesca. You give the others a heads up."

"Okay, thank you. We will send our husbands back later with a list," I said to the sales person.

We walked slowly, meandering in an out of gift shops to make it more difficult for him to follow. We wanted get a good look at him. On the way to the restaurant, we kept an eye out. However, I knew in my gut that it was him. I knew the others would want to know for sure.

Leaning in to me, Francesca whispered, "There's only one way to solve this. Give him a glimpse of the guys. Gina, come with me. I have an idea."

"We'll be back. You all have a drink and let them seat you at our table," she told the girls.

We circled back and could see Lil' Rocco sitting on a stool hiding behind a slot machine pretending to play.

Before anyone could ask what Francesca was thinking, we were gone.

Francesca and I stepped into the elevator, and the door closed.

"Halloween, three years ago," she said to me.

That was all she had to say. Brilliant idea, I only wish it had been mine, but that was what made all of us a good team. We usually knew what each other was thinking.

We had dressed up like our husbands for a Halloween party they had for their grandkids a few years back. Francesca and I dressed up in our husband's suits and the guys wore dresses. It was a riot. Everyone got a kick out of it.

We started working on her idea in the elevator as we headed back to our suites.

"It's the only way. He needs to see one of the guys," she continued as she put on one of Sally's suits.

She reached for his hat, put her hair up in it, and grabbed a cigar.

"Good thing I don't eat salads all the time," she laughed, rubbed her belly, and pulled the waistband of the pants. "Well, how do I look?" Francesca turned to face me.

I could not help but stare. You could see it was not Sally in the face, of course, but from a distance and from behind especially, wow. As long as we did not let Lil' Rocco get too close, it could work.

She was fully dressed.

"Well?" she asked.

"Scary good. First time I've ever been attracted to you," I said jokingly.

Hopefully, he would see us together and assume Sally and I were going to dinner.

We knew we had to stay close to him, but never in a clear shot. It was going to take some quick maneuvering.

"GiGi, give me a light," she said deeply as she held up her cigar to me.

She was totally in character. He would be able to smell the cigar. I lit her up and we were on our way.

"Now, when we get close, you say something loud in Sally's voice so he can hear you. I can look like him, but I cannot sound like him as much as you do. Let's get on a call so we can talk to each other. The girls can text us to let us know where he is. I will walk around the machines so he can get a glimpse of me. If he gets close to me, you can head him off. That's the plan. Got it?" she confirmed.

I texted Carlita to see if they could see him. They took turns going to the restroom on the casino floor to see if they could sneak around and get a glimpse of him. We definitely needed as many eyes on him as possible. Hopefully, he was alone.

The elevator doors open.

Ding

I receive a text from Carlita:

It's him...he's outside the restaurant on the third row of slots on the right hand side.

I texted back:

We see him.

We put in our new earpieces. We did not want him to see us on the phone.

We walked up behind him one row away.

"Bring me a Scotch with a splash of water over to the poker table, baby," I said as loud as I could to the server in Sally's voice.

We immediately left that row and ran around the corner. Francesca headed away from him towards the tables. I stepped back to watch. He jumped up and looked over the row of slot machines. He could smell the cigar. He came out to the end of the row and caught a glimpse of Francesca as she ducked into another row of slots. I stayed behind him so I knew where he was.

"He's coming. Go right. Two rows over," I told her.

He scrambled to find her.

Carlita sent a text:

Gina, he's turning around and coming straight for you. Quick, turn around.

We ducked right and weaved left. Francesca stood behind a machine so he could see the top of Sally's hat, then vanished in plain sight, at least his sight.

Lil' Rocco finally got up the nerve to yell, "Uncle Sally! Hey, Uncle Sally!"

Each time Rocco would get close, Francesca would run the other way. I went in the opposite direction and told her to drop the cigar. That way, he could not smell her trail and she could duck into the private high stakes poker room. As he got closer, we slithered in and pulled closed the long black velvet curtain behind us. We acted as if it was an accident. The poker room Pit Boss came over to us.

"Looking for a game tonight Sir?" he asked Francesca.

"Yes, but there will be five of us, and we would like a private room for the night." I said it so if Rocco was close by, he could hear us.

Carlita had been following Rocco. She watched him go out the door to the valet and drive away.

She came back in, walked through the curtain of the poker room, and said, "That was brilliant. He fell hook, line, and sinker. I can only imagine what that looked like with all of us running around the casino floor like we were kids playing hide and seek, but it worked."

The Pit Boss did not quite know what to think when Francesca raised her head and let her hair down out of the hat.

He smiled and said, "Alrighty then. I'm not even going to ask, but this night is going to get more interesting with you ladies, isn't it?"

I smiled at him and told him it was better he did not ask. We were going to have dinner and would be back to play some cards.

He introduced himself as Jax. He said he would get our table ready for after dinner.

Once we were certain Lil' Rocco was gone, Francesca peeled off from the rest of us to change out of Sally's suit.

We were sitting at our dinner table when Francesca returned in her own clothes. We clapped as she approached. It was a masterful performance and worthy of applause, maybe even an Oscar.

"All in a day's work. Right?" she asked as she took a bow and sat down.

Everyone reached for their glasses and held them up to toast the plan we pulled off brilliantly.

"To Gina and Francesca!" exclaimed Carlita.

"Cheers!" everyone retorted.

We enjoyed our dinner and ventured into to card room for a game of poker. We reveled in our accomplishment and creativity of the evening.

We stayed in the poker room for a while. We tipped well and bet low. Thank goodness, it was a slow night in the poker room. They probably would not have let us stay as long as they did. We finally gave up and headed back to our suites.

16. EVER HEAR OF A BRAZILIAN?

The next morning we slept in a bit. Once we woke and dressed, we decided to head over to the Scarlet Pearl Casino Resort in D'Iberville, Mississippi for the famous Jazz Brunch. I mean, who could go wrong with bottomless Mimosas and a Bloody Mary bar?

After brunch, it was time to get everything ready for the meeting with Lil' Rocco. We picked a small bed and breakfast called Coastal Oaks Bed & Breakfast in D'Iberville to meet him. We were able to rent all of the rooms, indefinitely.

The owner was Alphe's cousin, Judy. She was in the midst of beginning to remodel. There was only one guest, but he was scheduled to leave the next day. After that, the entire place would be empty.

As soon as we drove up, we knew it was the perfect location. No one would ever find us here. It was only a few miles from town, but it felt like the country. It had a long driveway full of mature trees and landscaping. It was small, but well-kept and charming.

Judy gave us all of the suites. We unpacked supplies and set up. We kept our suites at the Beau Rivage. We did not want to call unwanted attention, in case Lil' Rocco called the hotel. If he got suspicious, it would throw all of our plans down the drain.

We had the evening to unwind and relax. Alphe' and Alcide joined us. They were becoming like family. Judy served a great dinner. We sat under the lighted oaks while enjoying a few glasses of wine.

Alphe' began telling us about his afternoon of shopping. His face turned red from blushing. He said he had to Google some of the items so he knew what he was looking for. Finally, a sales associate came over to help him. He said the man asked if he wanted him to demonstrate how to use the hot wax on Alphe's leg. Everyone was laughing hysterically.

"I nearly ran out of the place without paying. I wasn't sure what any of that stuff was, but I be damned if I was going to let him show me," he said.

We continued to tell stories until we finished our wine. We headed back to the Beau Rivage for the night.

Morning came and we put our game faces on. Alphe' had all of our supplies and the limo out front waiting on schedule.

Now, all we had to do was wait for Lil' Rocco to show up for the 1:00 meeting. We were ready.

Everyone was watching the clock: 9:00 am, 11:00 am, 12:00, 12:05, 12:06.... Time seemed to slow down as it grew closer for Lil' Rocco to show up. Finally, it was almost 1:00.

"Adrianna, that's enough! We're just trying to knock him out, not kill him," Antonella yelled while grabbing the pills from her hand.

Adrianna was in charge of putting sleeping pills in the iced tea, so we could get him upstairs. She stirred very carefully, not spilling a drop and smiling the entire time. She looked like a mad scientist.

At 1:00 on the dot, there was a chime on the front door letting Judy know someone walked in. She greeted Lil' Rocco at the front reception area and led him into the meeting room. She brought in some iced tea and told him the guys called and were running late, but would be there shortly. She encouraged him to enjoy a glass of their favorite southern iced tea.

He was obviously nervous, tapping his nails on the table. He was not drinking his tea, so Judy went in and stuck an old-fashioned sugar cane stick in the tea.

"Try it with this. My uncle grows sugar cane back home. It makes it really good," she said.

She stood there looking at him, until he felt obligated to try her tea. Then, she smiled and walked out. He only had half a glass, but that was all it took. Two minutes later, his head was down on the table.

We went in to figure out how we were going to carry him up the stairs and to the suite waiting for him. Alphe' was standing guard outside the house to make sure no one showed up unexpectedly.

Judy said, "I'll help. I'm not sure what you're up to, but I'm in!"

We all looked at each other and smiled. She was shaping up to be our kind of girl, and we welcomed the help.

Lil' Rocco was only about one hundred eighty pounds, but it was dead weight. Fighting gravity going upstairs was hell.

Everyone grabbed a limb and started dragging him up the stairs. Half way up; his head dropped and hit one of the steps.

Judy said, "Oh no, I dropped his head. Sorry."

As she was lifting his head, it hit another step.

"That's okay," I said, and continued to pull upward.

"Okay, if you say so. This guy must have really done something terrible to y'all," she said as she let his head fall back and hit the next step and every step thereafter.

Laughter filled the stairwell as we continued to strain getting him to the top of the stairs. By the time we got to the top, we were dragging him up by his feet and legs with everything else dangling.

We let him hit the floor and took a break. Then, we dragged him the rest of the way with his arms following above his head.

We had to move fast. He only had a half glass of the spiked tea. We did not know how long he would be out.

We lifted him onto the king sized bed. We stripped him down to his boxers and tied his four limbs to the post of the bed.

"Whew! Damn Judy. Didn't you have a downstairs suite?" Francesca asked.

There was more laughter.

The light in the room was dim. Nothing was on but a bedside lamp on the nightstand to the right of the bed. The curtains were drawn.

Rocco started to wake up. He tried to pick up an arm, then a leg. He was groggy and went back to sleep.

He awoke a few minutes later repeating the same motions, first trying to lift an arm, then a leg, then another arm. After twenty minutes of his on again, off again consciousness, he finally lifted his head.

"Hello," he tried to yell, but was still too groggy.

Could he see our silhouettes across the room, or could he hear us breathing? Everyone was as quiet as a church mouse, anticipating what was going to happen next.

He lifted his head again and asked, "Hello, who's there? Boss, is that you?"

No one uttered a sound.

"Boss, are you there? Let me... what the hell... let me explain!" He yelled as he tried to raise his head and sit up.

It finally registered that he was not able to move.

"What's going on?" he confusingly asked.

Rocco noticed he was tied to the bed.

He called for Sally. "Boss, is that you? Uncle Sally? Luigi? Please answer me, I want to explain."

I stood up and slowly walked over to him. Carlita walked to the other side of the bed and turned on the light switch. Rocco could see the five of us surrounding the bed.

"What's going on? Aunt Gina, where's Uncle Sally?" he asked.

"You tell me. Where is Uncle Sally?" I replied

He looked at me, then to Carlita, Francesca, Antonella, Adrianna, and back to me. He was becoming more alert by the second.

Adrianna charged at him asking him what he had done.

I pulled her back. "I've got this Adrianna. I'll ask the questions."

I eased her back over to a chair.

Very calmly and in a soft tone I asked Lil' Rocco, "Why did you kill them? Who's behind this?"

"Kill them? Kill who? I did not kill anyone! I saw them! They got out!" he exclaimed.

We obviously did a good job convincing him they were still alive. He refused to believe they were dead.

The past few weeks flashed before his eyes. He immediately thought of the texts and calls. He realized he had not directly spoken with or seen them in person, except a quick glance in the casino. Maybe he did not see them. Was it them? His mind was racing and recalling every conference call and every short conversation he had since that day at Grosso's in New Orleans.

"Tell us what we want to know, or else," I said as I wrapped my hands around his throat.

Carlita nudged me. She gently pulled my hands from around his throat and pulled the covers back.

"So, they are gone?" he asked, looking around to each of us waiting for confirmation.

"Yes," I finally said. "Your little plan worked. But why? Why did you want them gone? Did you think that you could take over? You little turd. Do you think anyone would ever take orders from you? Who are you working with? I know you did not come up with this on your own. Tell me now, or else."

"Or else what? What do you think you're going to do? Once I tell everyone they're gone, I will be in charge," he said smiling and thinking he was tough.

Francesca said, "Well, maybe so, but we're in charge until then. You're going to tell us what we want to know."

Adrianna reached over to the left side and turned on the bedside table lamp. Rocco's eyes moved over to her. It looked like they were going to do surgery. There were strips of gauze, gloves, scissors, wipes, and a covered crock-pot. However, there were things he did not recognize, such as Kotex, tampons, and a bowl of clothespins. Adrianna lifted the lid from the pot and steam rushed out. His eyes got bigger. He wondered what we would use them for.

Adrianna taunted, "Lil' Rocco, did you know I went to beauty school when I was young?"

He looked at her with a *what the hell* does that have to do with anything look, but did not respond.

"No. You didn't know that," she continued, even though he had not uttered a word. "Well I did. We thought we could put some of my professional experience to good use. You see, we are not used to torturing people as you are... yet. So we are improvising."

Adrianna directed Antonella to start with the right leg.

Adrianna put on one glove and popped it on her skin for a dramatic effect. She put on the other and removed the lid from the pot. With a big spoon, she slowly stirred and lifted hot wax out. It stretched enough for Lil' Rocco to see what it was.

She pulled the sheet back to expose his legs, but kept his crotch area covered. She rubbed one of his legs and gave a little patch of hair a tug.

"Boy your legs are really hairy," she said as she walked over to the hot wax pot.

He laughed, "Ah ha! You think you are going to scare me with that? A bunch of girls?"

I reached over to the hot wax pot and turned it to the highest the temperature. You could see smoke billowing.

Francesca stepped back. "Do you think this is funny? Really? This is what women have to go through to look like this," she said, stuck out a leg, and waved her hand across her body.

Everyone giggled and I gave them a look. They were starting to have too much fun. I needed them to get serious. We needed answers.

Adrianna had a big glob of wax on her spoon and hovered it over his leg while it dripped.

"There we go," she said, as she smoothed it on his hairy leg

"OOOWWWWW!" Rocco startled before he could stop himself.

"Okay, how about this? Is it funny now?" she asked as she scooped another big spoon full and slathered down his leg.

"There we go. Let's smooth it all over so we don't miss a spot," she said sarcastically as she spread it back and forth slowly.

You would have thought she was buttering a piece of toast. Her animated face and smile gave away what was yet to come.

"AHHHHH, that feels nice. Thanks," he said, trying to match her sarcasm.

She said, "You're welcome and you're right. The wax usually feels nice after the initial shock of the heat, but I did not fully explain the whole process. Francesca, would you care to share the rest of the process with him. I do not want anything to be a surprise. I want him to know exactly what is coming next. Francesca, clothes pins."

Of course, Francesca was all too happy to oblige. She reached over and grabbed two clothespins. She then clipped his eyebrows to his eyelids making sure they stayed wide open. She made sure to explain each step. She placed cloth strips on the hot wax. She rubbed the strips so it would stick deep in the wax. She reached over to the other leg to rub the strips Adrianna had put on. She applied pressure, pushing up and down on his leg, more than necessary.

"There we go. Perfect. I have to rub those in good, so they get all of that hair. Now, we are going to pull off the strip all at once. We have to make sure it pulls every strand of hair on your legs out by the roots. Okay girls, everyone grab a strip," she said as she looked at us.

Rip!

Every part of Lil' Rocco's body straightened up, as if he was hit by a Taser or bolt of lightning. His face was as red as a beet.

He let out a huge scream. "Fuuuucccckkkk! Errrrrrrrgg!"

I was not sure what the second word was. It was more like a growl.

Francesca scolded, "Language, please. There are ladies present."

She then used a clothespin to clip his mouth shut.

"Good job girls! You see Roc, usually they pull them quick and it hurts less. But in your case, we want to make sure we get them all. Therefore, I will take my time. You know, once we pull the hair and root out, a lot may not even grow back. That is what we girls hope for. Anyways, here goes. Ready?" I asked, not waiting on an answer.

Antonella reached over to get more wax from the pot. "Whoops. Uh oh. I dropped some on his eyebrow and hair. That's going to leave a mark," she said playfully.

The wax was stuck in the clothespin, which was holding his eye open, and in his eyebrow.

"We don't want this to set in his eye," Antonella said.

She reached over for a tampon and stuck it to the running wax to stop it from dripping. Everyone laughed and backed away to leave the rest to the professional.

Adrianna pulled another strip.

He screamed and the clothespin popped off.

"Shit! What the hell! Stop!" Lil' Rocco yelled.

She pulled another.

He yelled, "Oh my God! How in hell do you do this? Why do you do this on purpose?"

I stepped up to answer, "We're a lot tougher than you give us credit for. Again Adrianna."

You could hear the hairs ripping from his leg.

"Owwwwwwww! Wait! Shit!" he yelled.

His breathing was heavy, and his teeth were gritted. His fists were so tight that his knuckles were white as snow.

"Here, bite down on this. It will help," Adrianna said as she placed a big Kotex pad in his mouth sideways.

It was the kind with the big belts. She clipped the belts in his hair.

I stepped up again to ask him if he was ready to cooperate. He shook his head no and mumbled under his breath. The only thing I could understand was something about him getting rid of all of us, as he did our husbands.

Carlita stepped up with some strips to put on the wax in his hair and eyebrow.

"Really? Looks like your eyebrows need a little shaping. Let me see if I can get the wax off that the rookie over there dropped on you," she said while winking at Antonella.

She pulled the strip off his eye.

"OOOWWWWWW!" he screamed with some other unintelligible words.

"I think he is speaking in tongues. Didn't really catch that. What was that?" I asked.

Carlita took off the whole eyebrow, except for a corner. Francesca reached over him to put a fresh tampon on it. She taped it around his head and hair.

"Carlita, you're really not very good at this either. Remind me to never let you do my eyebrows," I said.

Lil' Rocco was starting to sweat. He looked at us and did not say a word. I was not sure if he was holding his breath or if he was in too much pain to speak.

"Adrianna, maybe he can't take anymore. Get that wet towel and clean him up a bit. He has little blood blisters coming up all over him," I told her.

Adrianna was happy to do what I asked. She reached over to wipe the skin under his missing eyebrow.

He screamed bloody murder. "OWWWWW! You bitch! That is not water! That burns!"

"Oh no. You are right. I grabbed the alcohol by mistake. My bad," she said sarcastically.

I waited for something from him, anything. "Still nothing? Okay. Go ahead Adrianna. Let it rip! Literally."

Adrianna walked to the end of the bed. "Roc, ever hear of a Brazilian? Or a Manzilian? Those South American's can really come up with some great things. They love those little weenie bikinis, but they do not like hair. You are really going to enjoy this. Antonella, can you please Google the definition of a Brazilian or Manzilian wax for Roc?"

She answered, "Adrianna, I would love to, love to. Here we go. *Manzilian...the practice of male pubic hair removal. Male waxing is popular in the bodybuilding and modeling communities. Unlike the many styling possibilities for removal of female pubic hair, the male practice is mainly total removal, sometimes called the Manzilian, a contraction of male Brazilian.* Any questions?"

She reached over and pulled the sheet back further to expose his boxers and began to pull them down, but leaned over to have a peek.

Francesca grabbed another block of wax and threw it in the pot so he could see and hear it.

She leaned over Lil' Rocco and said, "Whoa! We are going to need a lot of wax down there. We are also going to need some tongs or something to hold that little thing up. I don't want to touch it."

Antonella reached over and grabbed the curling iron. She opened and closed the handle so it would hit the barrel each time.

"Will this work? It will definitely hold it in place," she said as she touched the barrel and winced at the heat. It had been heating for a while.

"Wait...Wait! You crazy bitches! Y'all are crazier than your husbands!" he shouted.

We smiled at one another, as if he had just paid us the greatest compliment.

He started singing like a canary. "I'll tell you what you want to know."

I put the lid back on the pot, and Adrianna took off her gloves. Antonella kept the curling iron visible to keep him on track.

"Okay, okay. It was not my idea. It was..." he stuttered.

"Who?" I yelled as I leaned over him with one hand on the lid to the hot wax pot and the other on the handle of the hot curling iron.

"It was Uncle Tony. He has been waiting for years to get them back for kicking him out of the family business," Lil' Rocco said reluctantly.

"Uncle Tony? Who's Tony?" Adrianna asked.

She had never heard of Uncle Tony. Adrianna was new to the family and did not know the stories of the past.

Carlita pulled Adrianna back so he could finish.

Uncle Tony had promised Lil' Rocco he could be his second in command. At first, it started out as a partnership. Then when Roc got cold feet, Uncle Tony threatened him. He told Rocco that if he did not follow through with killing the guys, he would meet the same fate.

"I had no choice. I swear! I was afraid," Lil' Rocco whined.

Antonella asked him why he did not go to anyone. He could have gone to Sally or any of the guys for help, but we knew they were growing tired of him. They probably would have gotten rid of him for even considering it or for talking to Uncle Tony.

Lil' Rocco cried out. "No. They would not have helped me! They did not trust me. They would have thought it was me. Uncle Sal would have killed me just like he did my Dad."

He was right. They did not trust him. Their instincts were right. They knew he was up to something, but did not know what. Missing money, anonymous warning calls, and frequent disappearing acts were his normal.

"You can sell this victim act to someone else, but not me. You could have gone to them. You chose not to. You wanted power and them out of your way. You'll pay for it," I told him.

I grabbed the masking tape and a Kotex Pad to tape his mouth.

"I don't want to hear anymore. Let's leave him alone for a while, until we figure out what to do with him," I said.

"Let's turn on *Lifetime Movie Network*. Let him listen to some chick flicks and get in touch with his feminine side a little more," Francesca said as she turned on the television.

The girls laughed and followed me out the door.

17.   PRETTY WOMAN

We went downstairs to figure out what to do next. We had to find Tony. So, I pulled Lil' Rocco's phone from my pocket.

"Surely he doesn't have him programmed in. He couldn't be that dumb," Carlita said.

"Well, never underestimate how dumb some people are. Here it is, Uncle Tony. He still has texts from him," I said.

The text read:

Rocco: *CALL ME*

Uncle Tony: *WHERE THE HELL ARE YOU???*

Rocco: *CALL ME NOW!*

Uncle Tony: *ROCCO, WHERE THE HELL ARE YOU?*

There were also eleven missed calls and six voicemails. I listened to the voicemails and they were not significant.

We couldn't call Uncle Tony or have Lil' Rocco call him either. All we could do was text him and set up a meeting. He would have him come to us.

Carlita typed in all caps on Lil' Rocco's phone:

YOU NEED TO COME TO BILOXI. I NEED TO MEET WITH YOU. THERE'S BEEN A NEW DEVELOPEMNT.

The phone rang immediately. Carlita answered while clearing her throat in a deep voice. Tony was screaming on the other end. She hung up and typed:

Bad signal here, come here and I'll explain everything.

She hit send.

A response from Uncle Tony immediately came back:

NO DAMMIT! EXPLAIN NOW! WHAT THE HELL IS GOING ON?!

She sent a text with the address and time to meet and left it at that. We knew if we ignored him, he would come.

We had a short amount of time to make a plan. Things were more serious than before. Dealing with Lil'

Rocco was one thing, but Uncle Tony was no one to play with.

I assured everyone I had a plan and began to share it.

"Wait. So who is Tony?" Adrianna asked.

I sat down and explained. "Tony is Sally's and Big Rocco's uncle. Uncle Tony was a bad ass. He was the Boss in every sense of the word. Big Rocco was smart, but he was a nice man. Uncle Tony wanted him to be tougher. Big Rocco tried to change things to make them run better, but Uncle Tony did not want change. When people started to listen to Big Rocco, Tony got rid of him. He did not care that he was his nephew. Sally swore he would take over someday and push out Uncle Tony for killing his big brother and he did. He disappeared before he could kill him. Until now, no one has heard from him, or so I thought. Looks like he's been trying to get back at everyone ever since."

Adrianna sat and took it all in.

I continued, "After he disappeared, they decided not to keep looking for him. They thought having him lose power and watch them take over the business would be worse punishment than being dead. After ten years, they assumed he was dead. I would have kept looking. I always thought he was alive and would come back some day for revenge, but the guys were not worried. I was not making the decisions then. I am now, and I will find him and kill him. I don't want to be looking over my shoulder like they did."

They sat in silence for a few minutes waiting for the plan.

"Did he start the business?" Adrianna asked.

"No," I said.

I explained further, "Before Uncle Tony took over; he was the right hand man to Gabriele Capone. He was with him for years, until Gabriele disappeared. The story is that Uncle Tony killed him.

The Capone family thought Uncle Tony would take care of them, but he did not. He double crossed them and took over everything. They lost everything. I never heard what became of Gabriele's kids or any of his family. I believe he had two boys and a little girl or maybe three boys. I really cannot remember the story. It was a long time ago. If memory serves me correctly, he had three or four kids though. Uncle Tony did not even send money to his wife, which was typical back then if you offed the husband.

Uncle Tony was ruthless. We definitely need to be ready in case he comes after us, but I doubt he will. He probably thinks we are too insignificant to bother with. He never put much value in women. He surely thinks he will cast us aside and take over without a fight from us."

I continued, "It's time to put an end to this once and for all. This is what we know. We know he is coming to us and he will be here tomorrow. We know we have to get rid of him. We know that Lil' Rocco has to go. What we do not know yet, is how. It is not as if we can just go in and shoot him. He would be ready for us the second we walked in the door. He knows us. We might be older, but you can believe that if he has been watching the guys, he has been watching us too."

"I could. I could just walk in and do whatever I wanted to him. He doesn't know me," Adrianna said with a wicked smile on her face.

All eyes turned to her to see how serious she was. She was right; he did not know who she was. I had to warn her again how dangerous he was.

Adrianna continued, "I want to do this. You can tell me everything I need to know to get me ready. He killed my Louie. He is old. How dangerous can he be?"

I reminded her of the fact that our husbands were gone. In itself, that was dangerous, old or not. If we were going to think about going after him, we needed to take him serious.

Adrianna was determined. I liked that about her. She had spunk. That is why Luigi fell in love with her. Most of his women were ditzy, but she was smart and had sass. She told me that she trusted she would be safe as long as we were there, and she was prepared.

I was nervous for her, but impressed by her fire. I figured this would be a good test to see if she had what it took to be one of us. Therefore, I agreed. However, I told her she had to do exactly what I said, and if I thought I needed to pull her out, I would.

"So now what?" I asked to myself, then aloud.

"He likes hookers," Francesca said quickly.

The girls giggled.

"That was random. Is that meant to be helpful or just some Uncle Tony trivia?" Adrianna asked.

Antonella chimed in, "He's old, but it must still work."

"Antonella, that's our in and exactly what I was thinking. Francesca, that's why I had Alphe' go out for this outfit and boots earlier," I said as I pulled out a few bags and handed them to Adrianna.

She grabbed the bags excitedly and pulled every piece out, one by one.

"I can do hooker. But wait, how did you know I would volunteer and that we were going to lure him here?" Adrianna asked.

All eyes turned to me

"Lucky guess," I said with a smile.

They were realizing I had been several chess moves ahead of everyone the entire time.

Adrianna stood up and slapped her hand on one hip.

"I'll channel my inner pretty woman. Does he look like Richard Gere?" she asked.

"Not quite, but we'll let you decide," Carlita replied.

We decided to cancel the Friday call. We didn't want to be forced to explain Lil' Rocco's absence. We sent out a text from Nico's phone:

No call this week. Working on some new business here on the Coast and we need Rocco here with us for a few days for meetings. Send your reports, and we will pick up next week for our regular call.

Texts came in acknowledging the text.

Everyone decided to stay the night at the B & B, but we did not check out of the Beau Rivage. We learned our lesson on that one from New Orleans.

We felt like we were as ready as could be. We all decided to retire to their rooms after dinner. I had a text message ding on my phone at dinner. I did not bother to look at it, until I was walking to my room. It was from Angelo.

It read: *Missed you today. Will ya'll be ready for a workout tomorrow?*

I could feel my face go flush, but something else caught my attention. Carlita and I heard music from the hallway. It was a piano. It peaked her interest more than mine. I continued to my room to read the text again.

Carlita stood in the doorway of the downstairs great room and saw Alphe' playing the grand piano in the corner. He was amazing. We could all hear it faintly from our rooms. No one minded. It was nice and calming.

Carlita sat behind him for a couple of songs. He did not know she was there, until she quietly walked over and sat on the bench next to him. He looked over at her and winked. She gently placed her head on his shoulder as he continued to play.

I came down after a bit to see what was going on. I did not make a sound. It was very sweet. This could be the start of something. I hurried back to my room. I did not want to disturb the moment they were having.

The sound of Alphe' playing took my mind off the day ahead and helped me drift off to sleep.

18. HE'S NO RICHARD GERE

It was Saturday. All of the girls were in a serious frame of mind.

Lil' Rocco's phone dinged with an incoming text message from Tony: *Be there in 2 hours. Where are you?*

Carlita immediately reached for the phone and typed: *Ok. There is a B & B north of Biloxi in D'Iberville. It's quiet, and I rented all of the rooms for privacy. Be at the bar at 5. I have a welcome gift waiting for you. I will be back tonight so we can have a late dinner.*

Uncle Tony texted back: *Okay.*

We made our plans and went over them, repeatedly. Everyone knew what they were supposed to do.

We all watched the clock intently: 3:00, 4:00, and 4:15. It seemed like time slowed the closer to 5:00 it got.

We were all in the kitchen area of the B & B. We anxiously paced a lot.

Finally, the front door opened and chimed as Uncle Tony walked in.

Judy went to the front desk to greet him. "Good evening, you must be Mr. Tony Madrina."
He grunted and did not seem to be very happy. He never was. Uncle Tony was seventy-eight. He was never a handsome man. He was tall with blonde hair. He had striking features with a strong jawline. He always looked grumpy, even when he was not. The last twenty-five years had taken a toll on him.

Judy made small talk. She asked him about his day and the weather, but did not get a whole lot of anything in return. She finished checking him in and brought him up to his suite. She opened the door.

"Looks like you've had a long day. Have a look around and freshen up. Rocco has a surprise that will be waiting for you in the bar at five. Come on down when you are ready. Call if you need anything," she said as she closed the door.

There was a light knock at the kitchen door where we were all waiting, with the exception of Alphe' and our

Pretty Woman. It was Judy reporting that Tony was in his room, and he would be down at five.

Alphe' called. He was on his way with Adrianna.

He had taken her away from the B&B, so it would look like he was dropping her off. We heard the car pull up. Everyone was glued to the window to get a glimpse of Adrianna.

She stepped out of the limo wearing high-heeled boots and a short skirt. She wore it well. She had on a halter-top with her back and belly showing. Her hair was down, and it was big.

Francesca stepped back and put her hands on her hips.

"I could have done the hooker thing. That outfit would have looked better on me," she said as she ate yet another fudge brownie Judy made. She was definitely a stress eater.

Everyone, of course, agreed with her.

"Francesca, if only Uncle Tony wouldn't have known you, you would've been the obvious choice," I said.

Judy smiled at Adrianna as she walked in the lobby. She was not smiling, and it seemed like she was not breathing either.

Judy walked over to her, leaned in, and whispered, "Breathe."

Then, in her regular voice she said, "You must be Rocco's friend. Let me show you to the bar."

"Breathe. We are all right here. Alphe' will be behind the bar. If you need anything, go to the restroom. Someone will come meet you," Judy assured her in another whisper.

Adrianna finally let out a big breath before she turned blue.

Judy took her to the bar area. Alphe' made her a martini and sat her down at the opposite end by the kitchen.

Uncle Tony walked in. Judy motioned for him to sit next to Adrianna at the bar.

"Mr. Madrina, I'd like to introduce you to umm, uh," she paused, as they forgot one major thing, an alias.

"Kit DeLuca. She is a friend of Rocco's," she recovered.

We all looked at each other in horror. I held my face in my hands. *OH MY GOD*, we could have blown the whole plan. Kit Deluca? What if he saw *Pretty Woman?* What if he knew the name and knew she was Julia Roberts' hooker best friend?

Judy stepped around to the back of the bar and said, "This is Alphe', he will be your bartender."

Alphe' was very charming and handsome. He had a New Orleans accent. His brown wavy hair and big brown eyes made for the trifecta.

"Can I get you a drink?" he asked. "We make the best sangria on the planet. How about a taste?"

"No, I'll have a cab. Bring a new bottle and I want it opened out here," Tony ordered.

Judy went into the kitchen followed by Alphe'. Alphe' returned with a fresh bottle of wine.

"Suspicious bastard," I whispered to Carlita sitting next to me behind the door.

Uncle Tony was no dummy. He was smart and paranoid, which was a bad combo for us. This one was going to be tough.

"That was close, great job with the name. I don't think he caught on. He seems too distracted, and I'm not sure he has even seen *Pretty Woman*," Francesca said to Judy.

There was no way she could slip anything into his wine. It was obvious we were going to have to use plan B. Adrianna will have to go to his room with him.

Uncle Tony and Adrianna was sitting next to each other at the bar and had not uttered a word. Uncle Tony did give her a once over from head to toe, but that was it.

"So, how long are you in town?" Adrianna finally asked, as if she did not know the answer.

She reached over and stroked the top of his hand with one finger, so not to get too close, but close enough to touch him.

"Couple days," he mumbled.

"A man of few words. I like that. No small talk. I am okay with that too. Talk is overrated," she said.

∞163∞

Adrianna took the olives out of her martini and reached over to feed one to him. It slipped out of her hand.

"Slippery little suckers," she shrugged and smiled. "I'll be right back. I'm going to the ladies room."

He nodded.

Alphe' was standing at the opposite end of the bar. He ducked into the kitchen to warn us that Adrianna may be losing it and that she went to the ladies room.

I snuck around the corner and into the ladies room with her.

"What's going on? Get it together. We are in this now. I wouldn't have let you do this if I didn't think you could pull it off," I sternly encouraged.

"I know, I know. Oh my God, slippery little suckers. I have *Pretty Woman* in my head. Get it together Adrianna," she said to me and to herself.

She checked her face, fluffed her hair, fixed her boobs in the tight little tank top, and turned to me for last second advice.

"You are going to have to get him up to his room. Since he asked for a new bottle, we could not put in anything to knock him out. Here are the pills. Put them in the bottle when you can. You'll have to take him upstairs to distract him," I advised.

"Okay. I can do this," she said as she walked out.

She came up behind him, leaned over his shoulder, and whispered in his ear, "So, do you have a nice room?"

Finally, she got a smile out of him.

Adrianna stood up and downed her martini. She took one of his hands and pulled him off the stool, while grabbing the bottle of wine with her free hand.

Tony opened the door to his room. Adrianna went in ahead of him, slipping the pills in the bottle while he was behind her. She picked up a glass and walked over to him to give him a refill. She put the bottle on the nightstand. She walked around to the front of the bed and sat down on the edge. She patted the bed next to her, as if to say *come sit here.* He moved toward her and sat.

She had to have been thinking, well, he's certainly no Richard Gere. I know all of us were. She got up, stood in front of him, and leaned down so all the cleavage stuffed into her miracle bra was in his face. She pushed him back on the bed, crawled over him, and kissed him on the cheek.

"I'll be right back. You make yourself comfortable. I've got something special to put on for you," Adrianna teased.

He nodded. He was still not saying much.

She went into the bathroom to change. She stood in front of the mirror looking at herself.

"Adrianna, get it together. What the hell am I doing?" she whispered to herself.

She folded her clothes nervously and put them on the bathroom counter. Her cellphone fell out of her pocket.

She picked it up and looked again in the mirror. She had an idea.

She continued whispering to herself. "I should record this in case something happens. Then, we will have evidence."

She hit record and stood the phone up on the counter, resting it under her clothes so the only part showing was the camera.

She could hear something going on. She peeked out the door. It was Tony rushing over to his suitcase. He pulled out his little blue pills. He opened the bottle so quickly that they all flew out. He picked up a handful off the floor and took one. He turned and looked at the bathroom door, made the sign of the cross, and took another. He guzzled his entire glass of wine, then reached for the bottle and took a big swig to make sure they went down. He jumped up and took everything off, with the exception of his boxers and socks. He slid under the covers in the bed.

The bathroom door flung open. Adrianna stood there in all black leather. She was holding handcuffs and a small tassel whip. His eyes were big. Finally, so was his smile. She stepped out of the door holding it so it stayed opened enough for the camera to have a clear shot of the bed.

She walked over to the bed twirling the handcuffs with one finger. She slapped the whip down on the bed, missing him by an inch. She swung one leg over him and sat on his legs facing him.

"You look like a man that's always in charge, but you're not in charge tonight," she said. "You're going to do exactly what I tell you to do, or else. And if you speak, I'm going to use these on you," she continued while holding the handcuffs. "Now get up and dance for me."

He had just turned seventy-eight and had a big belly.

"I don't think so," he said as he grabbed her, pulled her to him, and kissed her.

She pulled away and slapped the whip again. "You've been a bad boy. I did not say you could kiss me. So now, I have to follow through with my threat. Give me your hands."

Suddenly, he heard giggling. He lifted her off him, rushed to the door, and threw it open. No one was there. He looked down the hall and closed the door again. Everyone was listening outside the door and could not help but laugh at their very own *Pretty Woman*.

"Did you hear that?" Tony asked.

"No, I didn't hear a thing," she said loud enough for them to hear her.

"Just some other guests returning to their rooms, I'm sure. Now, where were we, I don't think I gave you permission to get up, now did I?" Adrianna said in a sultry stern voice.

He sat back down shaking his head.

She told him to give her his hands. He would only give her one hand. She cuffed him to one post of the iron bed. She knew she had to keep going, until she could tie him completely down. She walked over to the end of the bed and rolled down one stocking in slow motion.

"You want more?" she asked.

She rolled down the other and took them off. She took off the black leather skirt and had only bra and panties.

"More?" she asked again.

"Yes," he said.

"What will you do for me to get more?" she asked.

"Anything," he said with desperation in his voice.

"You may kill me, but that's okay. I have not been with a woman like you in years. It would be worth dying for," he said.

At that moment, he was too weak to fight her anymore. He was getting groggy.

"Okay. If you want more, than give me your other hand," she ordered.

He gladly raised his arm. She cuffed the other hand and jumped off him. She grabbed the whip and started whipping the hell out of him.

"Ow, that's too hard. Not that hard," he shouted.

"Not so rough," he said a little louder.

"Oh, I have only gotten started. Wait until you meet my friends. They like it rougher than I do," she warned.

"There's more of you? I don't think I can handle more," he admitted.

"Oh, I know you can't. There is no thinking to it. Girls, come on in. Uncle Tony is ready for you," she yelled as she walked over to the door opening it.

He shook his head and tried to focus. He knew something was wrong. He jerked his arms trying to free himself.

How did she know to call him Uncle Tony? Who was she and who were her friends she was calling for? Was Rocco setting him up? He had all kinds of questions and thoughts running through his head.

He kept jerking at the handcuffs. He was getting angry for allowing himself get into this position.

19. TRAINED CIRCUS MONKEYS

The door flew open. Carlita, Francesca, and Antonella walked in.

"What the hell? You bitch! Get me out of these things! I'll kill you!" Tony yelled.

I walked in last. I wanted to make a grand entrance.

"Good job Adrianna. Now, everyone grab his feet and tie those up too. Long time no see Uncle Tony. Damn. You look old. How long has it been? What? Fifteen years? Twenty? Twenty-five years? You should have stayed gone. I have to admit though, I didn't think you had it in you," I said smiling, as I grabbed the lamp shade from the small lamp on the bedside table and placed it over his boxers, which were standing straight up like a tent.

"I guess those little blue pills really do work," I joked.

Uncle Tony immediately began firing off questions.

"Where's Rocco? Where is Sally? What's going on with him to have his wife doing his dirty work now? I always knew he was weak. They all were," he ranted.

I asked the girls to get Lil' Rocco and bring him in for his meeting with Uncle Tony.

"Girls, go get Lil' Rocco. I believe they had a meeting scheduled. I will sit here and keep Uncle Tony company. Looks like he has something on his mind," I told them as I moved a chair closer.

He was still full of questions, but mainly trying to figure out where the guys were.

I leaned into him, face to face, and said softly, "Come on Uncle Tony. You really can't figure this out on your own? I am going to do to you what should have been done years ago. Since my husband isn't here too take care of you, I will."

"So they are dead? That damn Rocco is just like his worthless father. I knew he would screw this up? You won't kill me. You don't have it in you. You're housewives. Am I supposed to be afraid of you?" he said with every bit of arrogance he had left.

I smiled and backed away from him as the girls entered with Lil' Rocco tied to a wheelchair. Half of the hair on his body was gone. He was groggy. We kept giving him just enough to make him conscious.

"Damn. What happened to you?" Tony cringed looking at him.

"Don't ask," Rocco mumbled. "But I wouldn't make fun of them if I were you. These bitches are crazy!" he added.

Lil' Rocco had hair on one leg and small patches on the other. There were red blotches and blood blisters all over him. He had one eyebrow and small patches of hair gone from his head. He had a tampon taped to the other eyebrow with a clothespin sticking out of the cooled wax. He still had some cloth strips stuck in the wax, which they did not pull off because he begged them not to. Italians are known for being extra hairy, and he was the poster child for a hairy Italian.

"You're not going to get away with this," Uncle Tony said, still trying to maintain they were a joke, and he would be back in charge soon.

I can read people very well, probably better than Sally ever could. I knew Tony felt defeated, but his ego would never allow him to show fear. He would definitely not go down without a fight.

"Girls, take the hairless gorilla back to his room and swab those wounds with some alcohol pads. Wouldn't want him to die of an infection before we get rid of him ourselves. I need a minute with Tony," I ordered them.

I was good at being in charge. I always thought I would be a natural, and I was. It was important to me that Uncle Tony see me giving orders and the orders being obeyed. He had not been obeyed in a long time.

Uncle Tony mocked me. "Do you think pulling a little hair is going to scare me? Is that the best you've got? You think that you're going to get rid of us and take over? You are a joke. The guys won't take orders from a woman?"

He said laughing, "It will never happen."

"That's exactly what I'm going to do. Once they realize whom they have been taking orders from all this time, they are going to listen to me. Everyone has been taking orders from me, including you. You just didn't know it. You were so excited to get the anonymous tip that the guys would be in New Orleans. You started planning and did not bother to wonder where it came from. You lost your edge. You are not as sharp as you used to be, or you would have answered the question first. Well, it was me. I have been learning the business and paying attention to every little detail. Every now and then, I would let a little info slip about their business with Lil' Rocco, knowing it would get back to you. You see, I have been watching you for years and knew exactly where you were. I have been waiting patiently take over. This was my plan and you were just a small part. I was losing patience and thought I may have to kill the guys myself, but you played right into my hands. The whole family wants you dead. I will be a damn hero after this.

My husband was a great Boss, but he had been doing the same thing for too many years. He was set in his ways and did not want change. Unfortunately, I think that was the worst thing he got from you. That was his downfall. Even though he did not want to admit it, he had a lot of you in him. I've already made more money and made things run more efficient than you or he ever did," I said in a matter of fact tone.

"You don't understand. Pulling a few hairs out of someone legs will not get it done. There are things that have to happen, things you cannot even imagine. People have to disappear. People get hurt and get... dead. You think you're gonna be able to do that?" Tony asked.

"I guess you'll soon find out. Won't you?" I asked as I reached in the nightstand and took out the large roll of silver tape.

I tore off a small piece and covered his mouth. I unrolled another large strip, but did not tear it. I wrapped the strip around the back of his head and circled it a few times. I leaned over and tore the corner with my teeth, looking him in the eyes.

Sally used to say, "You have to look 'em in the eyes, no matter what."

"You see Uncle Tony, what you don't realize is you've been taking orders from me also. I knew one day you would get them, and I have been waiting patiently. I have learned the business and paid attention to every little detail. Every now and then, I would let a little info slip about their business with Lil' Rocco, knowing it would get back to you. I was losing patience and thought I may have to kill the guys myself, but you played right into my hands. I have known where you were the entire time you have been gone. I knew the little anonymous tip letting you know we were coming to New Orleans would get you right where I wanted you. Even if you didn't pull it off, my plan was to kill them and blame you anyways. That's why I always let Lil' Rocco think Sally killed his father. I knew you did. However, you had to have someone on the inside smart enough to help you, but dumb enough to think you could actually pull it off. You see, you and everyone else has done exactly what I wanted you to do, just like trained circus monkeys. Well, Rocco's a little less hairy monkey. I just need to tie up a few loose ends. Once I get rid of you and Rocco, there is no one the wiser. No one will ever know my part in this plan. So, you ask if I can do what is needed. Absofreakinlutely! I already have."

I paused.

"Bye Uncle Tony," I said and kissed him on the forehead. "At least you're going out on a high note." I lifted the lampshade and smiled.

I stood in the doorway and watched his eyes looking back at me, then turned and walked out. I went downstairs and told everyone that no one was to talk to Tony again. I told them I had taped his mouth and that we could not underestimate him. We needed to keep him tied up until we could get rid of him. We could not take any chances. I went upstairs and left the others in the kitchen.

I walked into Lil' Rocco's room with the roll of tape and sat on the bed next to him.

"You know, I was there the day you were born," I told him as I taped his mouth and wrapped it just as I did Tony's.

"I stood right next to your Mama, holding her hand until you got here. God rest her soul. She was a good woman," I said as I made the sign of the cross.

"If you would have only stayed loyal. Sally knew you were up to something, but could not bring himself to get rid of his big brother's baby. Me? I don't mind so much. I knew you could not be trusted. Tony played right into my hands, having you get rid of the guys, but you fell for all of his lies. Just FYI, he killed your father, not Sally. So I guess, you got played too. If it's any comfort, I will kill him first and you can watch. I am in charge now. It has to be this way. I am sorry. I wish things could be different, but I want to be in charge. I had to do things this way to make it happen. You were just part of my plan. Bye Baby," I said.

I walked over to the door and opened it. It was harder to have him looking back at me than Uncle Tony, but it had to be. He could not be trusted. He had proven that. Once they were gone and everyone knew I made it happen, I would get the respect the other Bosses received. I would make sure everyone knew.

20. BODIES, BAYS, & BAYOUS

I walked downstairs and into the kitchen where everyone was waiting.

"Alphe', please pull the car around. I'm ready to finish this," I said as I sat down at the table with the girls.

Alphe' and Alcide disappeared for a few minutes. Alcide returned to the kitchen.

"Gina, we're ready," he said.

Alphe' had already pulled the car around front and had it waiting for me. He and Alcide turned out to be tremendous assets. Alcide was a forward thinker, and we seemed to be on the same page.

It was dark outside. The moon was full, and the only other light was from the taillights on the limo. We walked around to the trunk of Alcide's limo. He opened it. Uncle Tony and Lil' Rocco were both tied inside. No one was around, so we could take our time. We sent Judy away in case things went bad.

Alphe' leaned in and whispered, "You sure you want to do this? This is not like waxing someone's legs. This is killing somebody. You can't take it back."

I knew you could not be in charge of an operation like this without being able to do whatever it takes to stay in control.

"They killed our husbands. They deserve it," I said.

Uncle Tony was squirming and grunting, trying to get someone to take off the tape. He tried to get everyone's attention, except mine. The girls were all curious to see what he had to say.

"Let's take this tape off to see if he has any final words," Francesca said walking over to the trunk.

I immediately stepped in front of her and stopped her.

"I've heard all I care to hear from both of them. All he wants to say is how no one will listen to girls. It is a waste of time. Alphe', close the trunk," I ordered.

All of the girls were standing around the trunk. I think everyone knew it was necessary. We were different people, ready to assume our new roles, and we were not afraid.

The girls got into the other limo and were about to pull away.

"Oh wait. I'll be right back," Adrianna said as she ran back into the front porch and through the front door of the B & B.

No one gave it a second thought. She ran upstairs and into Tony's room. Her clothes were still on the bathroom counter. As she picked them up, her phone fell to the floor. She had forgotten she was recording her hooker moment. She had not told anyone about it. It was a last minute decision before she went into the room with him, in case something went wrong.

She came running out and jumped into the limo with everyone else. She put her phone away and planned to share it later. Alphe' and I were still standing behind the limo, while everyone got in.

"Is that what all of this is about? Control? Are you planning on taking over permanently now?" Alphe' asked.

"Why not? I have been doing it. I have made changes and done things to improve the operation. Why? Do you have a problem with it or with taking orders from me?" I asked.

"No ma'am, not at all. I believe you can run the show. Maybe even the world." Alphe' said laughing.

"Good, because I want to teach you the business. I want you to take over New Orleans. We've recently had an opening down there." I said with a smirk and winked at him. "The girls will all be with me back home. I need someone on the ground here I can trust. That someone is you. The question is, do you have what it takes to do what needs to be done, no matter what that is, and can you take orders from women?" I asked.

He re-opened the truck and looked at Lil' Rocco and Uncle Tony, then back at me, "I carried them out and put them into the trunk. What do you think? Nope, none. I think I have been doing that the last few weeks pretty well, for most of my life for that matter. If you had known my Mama, you would understand that one. She was as tough as wet leather."

I welcomed Alphe' to the family and told him to finish this, as I pointed at the trunk.

He said, "The great thing about the South is the bodies of water. We have the Gulf, rivers, bays, and bayous. Things can get lost and never found."

"I did not want them to ever be seen again," I said.

"Okay Boss," he replied and smiled.

I said, "Alphe', call me GiGi.

21. IF LOOKS COULD KILL

We made it back to New York. It was time for The Godmothers to let the world know who was running the show.

I walked into Uncle Geno's and into the back room. I went early so I would be in the room alone. It was not dimly lit anymore, nor was there a trace of old wood paneling on the walls or tacky décor. It was now a beautiful, newly decorated, sleek room. The only familiar thing was the big round table our husbands and the Bosses before them, including Uncle Tony, had sat around for many years.

I sat down at the table and rubbed it with both hands. I smiled looking around and admiring our new room.

The table had scratches, dings, and initials carved in the wood. It reminded of when Sally and I were young. He secretly let me see the room. He was not in charge at that time. He was not even in line to be the Boss yet. I closed my eyes and could see it as clear as my hand before my face. The memory of when Sally and I were both in our early twenties and just married came flooding back.

He sat at the table, looked up at me, and said, "Baby, one day I'm going to be in charge of all of this."

He was gliding his hands across it, feeling all of the imperfections, just as I had done when I sat down for the first time.

I smiled, sat down next to him, looked him in the eyes, and said, "Me too!"

He laughed as if I had said the funniest thing he had ever heard. I was not laughing. I realized that moment I meant every word. He leaned down and kissed me on the nose in a condescending way. I have thought of that day many times over the years.

I opened my eyes and sat there as the rest of the girls came in. We settled in and talked about our first call. We looked around our beautiful new office with pride and excitement

It was time for our call, our first call as the Bosses, the top dogs, the Godmothers.

A bit later, a deep scruffy voice said, "Okay Uncle Geno, my girls are ready for lunch now."

It was Angelo.

He came in with lunch plates and placed them in front of the girls.

"Here you go, Babe," he said as he put my lunch down in front of me.

"See you tonight," he said as he winked and walked out.

Uncle Geno put the last dish down. He stepped back and looked around the room. He seemed happy about the changes to the office.

"Maybe you girls can help me redecorate the restaurant to look like this," he said playfully.

"Looks good. You girls are gonna shake things up around here," he said and closed the door behind him.

We were sitting around the table admiring each other and our new room.

I put my hand on the table, "Call me sentimental, but I couldn't get rid of the table."

They each smiled and rubbed the table as I had done. Some of the initials read SM, TM, GC, LC, and many more.

"So are we ready to do this as us?" I asked.

Carlita reached over to the center of the table and released the mute button on the new intercom phone. We could hear everyone else as they connected to the call. Adrianna rubbed her hand over the LC thinking of Luigi and looking at the GC next to his initials. All of the initials had a thousand stories that went along with them.

Adrianna had her phone sitting on the table in front of her. She grabbed it to turn off the ringer. As she set it back down, her photos opened by accident. She noticed the video of her hooker moment with Uncle Tony. She realized she had never watched it. She slipped her ear bud in one ear and hit play. She would share it with everyone for fun after the call, but wanted to take a quick peek to admire her breakout performance.

Carlita spoke, "Gentlemen are we ready to get started?"

"Yes Ma'am," Neely said.

"Yes Boss," Alphe' answered.

Everyone else followed suit.

Adrianna participated in the call, but also watched the video, trying to keep the smile off her face. She thought it was over, until she saw me sit next to Uncle Tony. She continued to watch and heard everything I told Uncle Tony. She heard me admit I was responsible for everything. She was watching in disbelief. She had cold chills and the hair on her arm was standing up.

She heard me say, "You see Uncle Tony, what you don't realize is, you've been taking orders from me also. I knew one day you would get them, and I have been waiting patiently. I learned the business and payed attention to every little detail. Every now and then, I would let a little info slip about their business with Lil' Rocco, knowing it would get back to you. I was losing patience and thought I may have to kill the guys myself, but you played right into my hands. I have known where you were the entire time you have been gone. I knew the little anonymous tip letting you know we were coming to New Orleans would get you right where I wanted you. Even if you didn't pull it off, my plan was to kill them and blame you anyways. That's why I always let Lil' Rocco think Sally killed his father. I knew you did. However, you had to have someone on the inside smart enough to help you, but dumb enough to think you could actually pull it off. You see, you and everyone else has done exactly what I wanted you to do, just like trained circus monkeys. Well, Rocco's a little less hairy monkey. I just need to tie up a few loose ends. Once I get rid of you and Rocco, there is no one the wiser. No one will ever know my part in this plan. So, you ask if I can do what is needed. Absofreakinlutely! I already have."

Adrianna kept backing up the video. I looked over at her several times to get her attention, but could not. I had no idea what she was doing. All I could see was her playing on her phone.

She was being asked a question from one of the guys on the speakerphone.

"Adrianna. Adrianna," Carlita said several times, trying to get her attention.

She looked up from her phone not to answer the question, but to look straight at me... with a look that could kill.